On Rules

an anthology

ON RULES

Published by Unleash Press

Reynoldsburg, OH 43068

unleashcreatives.net/press

Copyright © 2024 by Unleash Press

Book Cover by Christopher Shanahan

Edited by Ashley Holloway and Jen Knox

Printed in the United States of America

ISBN 979-8-8692-2485-9

Contents

ON RULES

Johnathan Chibuike Ukah

Winner, Editors' Choice Prize

A short interview with the author can be found at the end of the anthology. From the author: *"Poetry is also the source of music and without music this life would be a graveyard."*

Jonathan Chibuike Ukah writes poetry from London where he lives with his family. His poems have been featured in *Strange Horizons, Atticus Review, Unleash Lit, The Pierian, The Journal of Undiscovered Poets* and elsewhere. He has received Pushcart Prize nominations and literary prizes.

ON RULES

My Daughter

Tomorrow, when they ask me
about my answer to the restlessness of life;
when they question me about living
and how I was able to reverse their affliction
into spears, bullets, wasps and snakes
chasing them from the paradise they took from me,
into the valley of bones and blood,
I would give them this answer.

I would show them how I sent you,
and you stood in their midst as an illusion
to discover the things they hid from me;
to reveal the secrets they squatted on,
while fakery caged their hearts;
I would show them how they mortgaged grace,
and propped up their vanity on their spurious feet,
and how my hunger for the truth grew like mushrooms.

You, whom they rejected, whom they neglected;
You—they tried to clip your wings
with the little scissors in their handbags;
you whom they forgot to follow
the same way a dog follows a goat with dysentery.
When they saw you grow beautiful and wise,
they fidgeted within their bones
and pulled their teeth with a chisel.

ON RULES

My Brother's Martini

My brother and I were born in a little town
which was the last to die of bombs,
after the army had declared No Victor,
and No Vanquished.
Our city grew on a plantation of mushrooms,
which the Nigerian soldiers did not conquer
or did not consider defeating.
There is no heroism in slashing the heads of vegetables.
The language of the mushroom was nervy,
and they did not wish to bother their tired minds
with the alphabets of the Cassava War.
Speaking of that war in the 30s was taboo
in a country that attempted to murder memory,
yet it was the silence of the mushroom
which made memories living today,
which painted the tapestry of bombs and guns
that were the means of decapitating destinies.
I did my best in the circumstances
to preserve my brother's inheritance
in the share of our joint pain and despair,
so that his dreams of keeping memories alive
would flourish within the blades and veins
of mushrooms growing in our fingers.
Though I often wondered how long it would take
for the gods of my father to start throwing bombs

in the name of fighting their internecine wars.

The silence of the teeming red termites,
the ants of the anthills of the Savanna,
the undying terrain of green vegetation,
the cocoa plantation near our house,
where snakes and spiders waited with flowers
to offer to us as souvenirs for survival,
the pumpkin leaves, uha and hibiscus,
the colony of dandelions and magnolias,
lilies, roses, chrysanthemums,
where cicadas and butterflies hid from flies
sheltering in the fields of corn and yams,
where nothing was extraordinary
except for their powers of showing weakness
that made enormous strength possible.
It was the unavoidance of the victory of the weak
that made the strength of the strong an illusion.
The soldiers ignored the mushrooms
where my brother and I found a fraternity,
and cut down the towering Iroko trees
believing that their unbroken barks
formed the bastions of their versions of crime.
We survived this war in our backyard
with the broken dishes and plants rubble.

That's how my brother and I separated,

ON RULES

and absconded from our land,
at the age of fighting for the longevity
of our uncommon dreams, our united survival,
having decided that there would be no empire
built together as children of the city of rubble.
We went our separate ways,
sheathed our youthful weapons,
to live in foreign lands where ageing was fruit,
and peace the nucleus of dreams;
our destiny intertwined with our trauma.
Our parents did not realise this debacle,
until we wrote to them from our different hideouts.
The gaps in our years fostered my brother's dream
of uniting with me in an age where there was no war,
though such thoughts were cacophonous
when our city lay a sprawling rubble,
a landscape of pain and sorrow,
destruction and frustration, despair and grief,
where death was not the unwieldy killing,
but the inferno and ruination of bodies
that made it unassailable to memory.
We were a generation of the dying
without the permission and freedom to return
to remember and mourn the lost age of war,
joy without celebration, victory without conquest.

My brother and I reunited at last,

ON RULES

after many years of cloudless skies
as prisoners of an openly silent war
that made fighting with Ogbunigwe impossible.
He had grown up tall and weak;
a bowl of lickable hot soup
steaming inside without the poise to boil over,
or the bones to bubble up and spill into the fire.
He was still a young man of promise,
brimming with dreams of reconstructing
the vertical to the horizontal,
turning a moment of grace into an eternal blessing
or to be the bending Iroko that stands firm
and not the resisting oak that has no spinal cords.
We were children of the sky once,
but now walking tall with our heads lowered,
our eyes are a picture of the same despair
that drove us out like the rat in a rabbit's hole.
The same unanswered question is in our hearts.
He arrived with his wife with a bottle of Martini
which had no alcohol in its dictionary.
And I was left to wonder at the riff in our memories
which carved out defeat as not belonging to victory
a personal best performance in the battle for existence.
It was the only response we achieved from time
when our brows grew mould and our eyes darker,
when our faces wore the tiredness of a fight
that had taken a toll on our minds;

ON RULES

like the undying and the undead
slumped in the valley of dry dreams and bones.
His wife offered us a bouquet of love and peace
unmixed with the dream of walking on a tapestry of bombs.

ON RULES

A short interview with Jen Knox

Jonathan, please tell us a little about your writing process and purpose.

My writing process begins with inspiration. This can happen anywhere I am. On the bus to work, on the street walking around, in bed before I go to bed, just anywhere. I have my mobile phone ready for writing at any time. My iPhone has an excellent writing pad which I have been using for a long time. Most of my poems start from there before ending up on my laptop.

Inspiration has no restriction. It affords me the reason to write by providing me with an issue to write about. The Exception is if I have a writing prompt. In that case, I will ask for the visit of inspiration or I go out searching for it through research. I read poetry books, poems online and listen to poetry podcasts. If I write the poem on my iPhone, I will send it to my email later, download it later, edit and edit again. My editing process is limitless and I write at least a poem a day.

Can you speak to what you believe poetry offers the world?

Poetry has so many things to offer the world. It offers empathy with one another. it comforts those who mourn; those who suffer from tragedy or loss, those who feel lonely and deserted, those who feel abandoned. Poetry is solace. Within its amber is hope; within its words is integrity. Through poetry enemies can mingle and become friends again. Its usefulness is boundless. It serves other purposes like endeavouring to correct the ills of society by drawing our attention to them. The poet is a visionary and can prophesy about the future if the ills are not corrected. Poetry is also the source of music and without music this life would be a graveyard.

Why poetry, specifically? And how did you begin as a poet?

Before I started writing poetry, I was into fiction. It took me about three or four years to write a novel. By then the message may have expired and the purpose defeated in a fast-moving world like ours. But poetry requires only a few words to send the message. It works like a telegram, quick, brief and poignant. I started writing poetry from the time I was in secondary school, though I did not fully understand why I loved some sections of the Bible like Psalms, Proverbs and Ecclesiastes. The poetic nature of the Bible gave me my first insight into a world different from the trauma of bullying and abuse which I suffered while I was in Secondary School in Nigeria. Writing poetry comes naturally to me, unlike fiction, and it helps me a lot to process grief and the effects of the civil war in Nigeria, 1967-1970. Biafra suffered human and material losses as a result of it.

Thank you, Jonathan.

Lareina Abbott

Lareina Abbott pens Métis themed speculative fiction, essays and memoir. Her stories have a tie to the spiritual or natural world, and to ancestry, as she believes that these connections are how we will heal as a people and reclaim what has been previously lost. She received the 2023 Howard O'Hagan Short Story award for her short story "Ma Soeur Marie" published in the *Prairie Witch Anthology* and was part of the 2023 Audible Indigenous Writers Circle. She originates from a cattle ranch in northern British Columbia but currently lives and writes in Calgary on Métis Local 87 and Treaty 7 territory.

ON RULES

Crooked

Let me tell you a story. The story of the crookedness of my family. We are so bent that when a new situation arises, we easily fit into it, crooked like the shape of newness. We bend with the river; in fact, we enjoy it, this new shape, the new place, the new experience. But crookedness has a price. There are places in this world that don't like the crookedness of us.

These places are cities, towns, places with rules. Stupid rules. Some people in the world right now are angry about too many rules, and I'm not agreeing with those people; my agreement would depend on the rule, and the people. I know that one person's idea of a stupid rule is another person's safety. The rules I speak of are the rules that changed how people thought of us, without anything changing about us at all. They were the rules of colonization. The rules that turned us from "The people who know themselves" to "The people who should be ashamed of themselves".

My granddad was a white guy and so you might say, why the heck are you writing about him, he wasn't Métis? Wasn't he one of the colonizers? He was born in England but was picked up and moved to Northern Alberta when he was a kid without so much as a 'see you later.' His family lived in Lac La Biche, and despite being a white boy, he grew up like a Métis boy: he trapped, smoked the pipe with the Métis men, spoke Cree. To hear my grandmother tell it, he was more Métis than she was. What was it to be Métis, you ask? It was to be resourceful, and not just that, to do it with a grin and a gleam in your eye. A love of music and humour, a wink and a nod. Have you ever met a Métis person that was not charming? Are you one of those unsuspecting souls who have had your heart taken away by a Métis man or woman? Well it's not their fault, it's in their blood, they just can't help it, you see. The trickster lives in them, always trying to find a way out. Just

ON RULES

like the French voyageurs that were the fathers of our Métis nation, my granddad was like-hearted.

Anyways, my granddad was as crooked as they come, which is to say that he could find his way around a problem. He was resourceful and charming; he could dance a mean jig, so they say. I never met him and he never met me, but through all the hard times, even after he had died, there was still the sense of that man's influence on our family, that resourceful man. I've only learned these things about him recently. You see, the existence of my un-talked about grandparents is like a family black hole, you are somehow pulled into their sphere of gravity, but you never have a clear view of them. It's only been lately that I have begun asking the questions: "Tell me about my mom's dad; what was he like?" Afterwards I would be left with a vague impression that was immediately forgotten, and I wondered if I had even asked the question. But I've learned to ask stronger questions, more persistent questions.

I have a black and white picture of my grandparents standing next to a car. The kind of car that was made right, with pure steel, a car that gave you confidence when you drove. He looks like Buddy Holly: big glasses, serious face, and a short sleeve polyester shirt. He's leaning against the car. She looks like every other woman from the 50's, just like you see in movies with Elvis, a wide skirt and a thin buttoned sweater and flats. The only difference being that instead of a blond ponytail and sparkling blue eyes, like all the girls in the movies, my grandmother has the Métis—dark eyes, dark wavy hair, and easily tanned skin that I inherited from her.

What does this have to do with being crooked? Well, let me get to that.

ON RULES

I found out my grandmother fell in love with my granddad because he could dance. Dancing with a Métis man is like wanting to touch lava—it gives you such a deep longing that you can't help what you do next even if you know it's not good for you. I imagine the heat that flowed between them when they danced. In Lac La Biche, they got married, had four kids, and lived in a little house with mud floors across the lake, across the river. Life in Lac La Biche was a life without bills; you solved your own problems, found your own food, repaired your own house. It was a life for those who were resourceful and my family thrived. My granddad had a mink farm, but one year there was a fish shortage, and he fed the mink with suckers from the pond. All of the mink died, and my granddad had to go find work. The year was 1948 when he left with a friend to find work on the Pacific coast as a commercial fisherman, but they stopped in Kimberley, BC to stay with his sister-in-law, and he never left.

My granddad chose a spot in the valley below the railway for his house. Have you ever been to Kimberley? A town between mountain ranges, the pines tower darkly on the hills, underneath god skies. Down from the town proper, he built the house next to the pulp mill with salvaged railway ties. My grandmother and the kids joined him, and they became town people.

But life in town wasn't a fit for a proud and resourceful trapper family. With one eye lost in a hunting accident years before, Granddad couldn't get work in the mine, so he became resourceful.

I've always been proud of my family's ability for resilience. I've had wonderful life adventures, despite a lack of experience or money. We've all had lives beyond what others think we should've been allowed. I've travelled the world, have a doctorate degree, and live a beautiful life. But I owe my life to my ability to bend. Growing up in

ON RULES

Northern British Columbia, in Fort St. John, we used to go to the dump to look for 'treasures.' Before Kijiji, before eBay, there was the dump. My family were the garage sale kings. We would go to Edmonton on vacation and spend our time going to garage sales in wealthy parts of the city. There was always this feeling that we had pulled one over on the people who had paid full price, like we were in on a secret.

That was how I imagine my granddad felt, when he started going to the dump to harvest copper. That copper made it so they could live, and it provided the extra money for a billed existence. One year, my mom, who was still under ten years old, found a special gift under the Christmas tree, a gift paid for in copper. It was an accordion, a huge expense for her parents.

My family was proud; they didn't take any handouts from anyone. But when the police came to take my granddad away, their resourcefulness and my granddad's copper harvesting became a strength that the 'rules' used against them.

John Peter Beck

"I was originally raised in Michigan's Upper Peninsula in the lake town of Escanaba. I have been on the faculty of Michigan State University's Labor Education Program for over three decades. At MSU, I co-direct a program on workers culture, Our Daily Work/Our Daily Lives, at the MSU Museum. My poetry has been published by *The Louisville Review*, *The Seattle Review*, *Passages North* and *Another Chicago Magazine* among others."

The Handling of Tools

"The handling of, and accounting for, fools (sp) was in conformity with Federal regulations."
*(Draft manuscript of the Report of activities and accomplishments of the Civil Works
Administration in Michigan [November 1933 - March 1934])*

They are useless
when dull;

it pays
to keep them

sharp.

Common sense
is the best rule

when employing them.
They should always

be put
in their proper place.

It may seem pointless
to count them all,

but a strict accounting
is required.

Dr. Deidra Dees

Like her father before her, Dr. Deidra Suwanee Dees grew up picking cotton in rural Alabama. She and her family descend from Hotvlkvlke (Wind Clan) following Mvskoke stompdance traditions. She is the author of the chapbook, *Vision Lines: Native American Decolonizing Literature*. A Cornell and Harvard graduate, she serves as Director/Tribal Archivist at the Poarch Band of Creek Indians where she lives with her family including rescue puppies. She teaches Native American Studies at University of South Alabama. Heleswv heres, mvto.

ON RULES

Excerpts from *Indian Ice: Indigenous Witness / Estv-Cate' Het'ute*

Mvskoke Record

Author's note: Otis Dees (1917-1984) kept a record of his school years, shared by his daughter. The record ends here because the Great Depression caused such deep poverty that Otis Dees, along with many other children of the era, had to drop out of school to go to work to support his family.

First Grade

September 18, 1923

When school was over at the one-room schoolhouse, I grabbed Birdie's hand and we headed for home. We ran and we ran and we ran, trying to get past the white boys, 'cause they all laugh at us and beat us up when they can catch us. The white boys say we're no good 'cause we're Mvskoke Indians.

Robert Davis said he was gonna take me behind the schoolhouse tomorrow and scalp me! I told the teacher when Billy Ray said the same thing last week, but *she's white too.* So she didn't do nothin' about it, of course. I don't think she likes me, neither.

As we ran past John Gulsby's house, he yelled so everybody can hear, "Otis Dees is a poor Indian Redskin!" I told Birdie to try and keep up with me, and I ran faster than I thought I could.

ON RULES

When we got home, me and Birdie got a drink of *cooold* water in a big giant dipper from the well. Then we fed the chickens and the cow. Mama told me to ring a chicken for supper, but *Birdie-had-to-cook-it; Birdie-had-to-cook-it.* Mama couldn't cook 'cause she was too sickly to get out of bed. I think she might be gonna have a baby or some kind of grown up stuff like that.

Second Grade

October 8, 1924

Daddy broke his hip last spring when the mule bucked the plow when he was plantin' cotton. Now I gotta do all the work on the farm. I just wish I can get paid for it. But I'm old enough to know that Indians *ain't got no money*.

December 10, 1924

"Otis, *Otis!* Come here, *Otis!*" Mama hollered. I knew she had something for me to do from that calling. I climbed down from the dogwood where me and Berdie was climbing up to the top, and I ran in the kitchen to see what she wanted. "You take this sugar to Coosah, *Otis*, okay*?* You feed *all this sugar to the horse—you hear me?"*

"Yes ma'am," I told her, intending to do what she said. As I headed to the barn, my nose caught a scent of the molasses sugar in my hand. I thought how good that sugar would taste! Like candy the white children brought to school in their lunch pails. Like lollipops in The Big Store that Indians can't afford.

ON RULES

When I was out of eye-shot of Mama, I pushed my face right in the pile of sugar and took the biggest bite I could get. Rocky, gritty, then melting like syrup, sliding down my throat—sugar rush.

I shoved my hand under Coosa's mouth. "Here's your sugar, ole boy," I told him. "Pretty boy, gentle boy." I rubbed Coosah's face while he was nibbling and slobbering.

He looked up and nudged the side of my head, wetting my hair. It looked like he was asking me, "Where's the rest of my sugar?"

I halfway ducked, caught myself. I really shouldn't be bothered by Coosah's slobber. After all, I guess it was a small price to pay for stealing the horse's sugar.

Third Grade

November 18, 1925

Daddy looks more sickly than I ever saw him. He told me Mama had two babies last night. He said the negro midwife, Ms. Della, tried to help but the babies *both died.* Daddy said it was kindly strange that while he was sleepin' in front of the fireplace, a haint[1] that looked like a fireball woke him up, and shot up from between his toes and went up the chimney. And that was the same time that the babies died.

February 19, 1926

ON RULES

Joey Cramer who goes to school with me—his mama said she was tired of all that politicking going on down there at the white church. She came over last Sunday and picked me up by the arm and slung me up in the back of the wagon with Joey, and off we went to the whiteman's church. Some of the men made me sit on the floor 'cause they said Indians ain't allowed to sit on the benches with whites. That made Ms. Cramer as mad as a hornet. But we sit on the floor all the time at home, so I didn't pay them no never-mind.

The preacher told a story about a baby that was born in a faraway land. He said the baby was born to die so all the people can go up to heaven... *even Indians*. He told all the people who wanted to go up to heaven to go up to the front. I ran up to the front of the church house and I said, "Preacher man, Preacher man, I wanna ask baby Jesus to take me to heaven."

But it didn't do me no good. You see, Ms. Cramer caught that TB[2] that was goin' around and she died that winter, and that ended that. I don't care nothin' about going to the whiteman's church anyhow, so I didn't pay them no never-mind.

Fourth Grade

September 22, 1926

I wanna learn some schoolin' but I just can't catch up to the fifth graders. I wish I can read as fast as them. My oldest sister Ruby always says I should be thankful for gettin' to go to the whiteman's school. Sometimes I get tired of hearin' her say it, and I don't pay her no never-mind. The government didn't pass the law so Indians can go to school until

ON RULES

Ruby was eleven. She must of caught up 'cause she's in ninth grade now. She sits in the desk on last row with tenth- and eleventh-graders.

My cousins Jesse and Wesley said we could come over to play last Saturday. I'm glad they did 'cause I wouldn't have nobody to play football with. Me and Berdie went over to Jesse and Wesley's and we played football all day long. On accident, I hit Jesse in the head with the football, and I know his mamma's gonna whup me when she sees his black eye.

Joey Cramer and some sixth graders let me play marbles with them this morning at school. The reason why is they wanted *my marbles* that Jesse gave me. But *I won their marbles!* I don't expect they'll be asking me to play again.

Fifth Grade

December 12, 1927

Mama's still kindly sickly, but she's goin' vistin' Aunt Queenie in the big city down in Mobile. I helped her hook up Coosah to the wagon to go catch the train for her trip.

I earned twenty-five cents last week pickin' cotton for old man Gladshaw. I was savin' it up to get a second-hand football. But mama asked if she can borrow it for her trip, so... I gave it to her.

December 21, 1927

ON RULES

When I came in from school today, Daddy told me Mama died... in Atmore.... coming back from Aunt Queenie's. The whiteman at the train station told Daddy he wanted to take Mama to the hospital but Indians ain't allowed in the hospital. He said Mama died right there in the train car.

I'm scared.

I'm glad I lent her my twenty-five cents. I don't mind now that I'll never get it back.

Right after Daddy told me about Mamma, visitors come up in the front yard, and me and Birdie ran under the house to hide. We don't know all the people what come, but they said they was our relatives. I never seen so many Mvskoke Indians in *all my life*. Daddy seen us hidin' through the cracks in the floor, and made us come out from under the house. He said we had to have a proper introduction to our relatives.

It didn't bother me before, but now it's hard for me to think about disobeying Mama when I stold Coosah's sugar. I think that was the only time—*the only time*—I ever disobeyed Mama.

Sixth Grade

September 28, 1928

Jack Kindle, who lives behind us, said one of the boys down the road got an indoor outhouse. I don't figure I'd want one of those due to the bad smell. Ain't nothing wrong with our outhouse. Only thing is—it's a long ways to walk at night when it's cold and I don't like usin' no slop jar.

There's some negro boys that live across Dees Creek behind us, where Ms. Della lives, and they came across the creek today. I hid in the bushes so as I can get a good look at 'em. The teacher said, "Don't go near them 'cause, if they touch you, your skin will turn black as soot." I took a good close look at them boys and there weren't a one of 'em black—they was all kinda brownish color like me.

January 18, 1929

A whiteman rode his horse from the county seat to our house with saddle bags full of papers. He told us we gotta get new birth certificates on account of the fire that burned the courthouse down in September. He said all the papers inside burnt clean up. But Daddy said birth papers ain't important to Indians. That's something the whiteman made up just to find out how many of us there is. So we didn't pay him no nevermind.

Seventh Grade

November 25, 1929

Johnny Blacksher goes to school with me. His mama cooked some fried fish, and said I can come over and eat dinner with 'em on Sunday. I wondered why—'cause *they ain't Indians.* They had the best fish and everything—mashed potatoes, sliced tomatoes, fried okra—kinda like Mama used to make. Johnny's mama even gave us a Coca-Cola in a see-through glass bottle. Since the big stock market crash, a lot of people can't buy things like that. We ain't ever afforded 'em. Daddy says they ain't no good for you no way.

Daddy asked if the fish was from the ocean in the Gulf of Mexico, the saltwater kind. I told him Johnny said his uncle caught the fish in the Alabama River near the bluff where Red Eagle and his horse jumped into the river to keep from being killed in the Red Stick War.

Daddy said, "You shouldn't *never* eat that saltwater fish."

He said one time he went to town and saw a peddler who had some saltwater fish on sale. It was all the fish you can eat for five cents. Daddy said it would of been a good deal, but he couldn't eat none of that fish on account of it being too salty.

Eighth Grade

November 29, 1930

When I came in from huntin' today at almost dark, there was two horses hitched to two wagons in the front yard and one automobile. We ain't never had no automobile in our yard before. One of the wagons was like the covered wagons, like the Wild, Wild West kind. Like the kind the cowboys says the Indians shot up with arrows for no blame reason. They're just ignor't and they don't know anything. But the cowboys—stealing our land, and taking our food, and changing us to poor Indian trash—sounds like a good enough reason to me to shoot 'em all slap up.

ON RULES

When I went inside to see what all was going on, Ruby met me at the door and told me Daddy had died. I know Daddy was very sickly for a long time, just like Mama. Birdie was in a awful way. Our relatives came to get him ready for the funeral. Daddy was lying on his and Mama's bed. I'm fourteen now and I'm supposed to be a man about it. But I swear I had to get away from the house and go in the woods and just *let loose*. I especially didn't wanna let Birdie see me cryin'. Indians ain't allowed to cry.

Ninth Grade

<u>September 1, 1931</u>

They built a new schoolhouse 'cause the old one burned down last summer. The new one's got lots of rooms and it's built out of red bricks. It's even two stories high with upstairs classrooms.

Now that I'm in ninth grade, the white boys don't pick on me half as badly. I think it's 'cause I grew bigger than all of 'em. They quit fighting me 'cause I started winning.

Tenth Grade

<u>December 7, 1932</u>

I'm playing high school football for the Blacksher Bulldogs. We're beatin' all the schools in the South. I got my first football letter at the end of last season. All the white boys call me Square Dees 'cause they say I can knock a square hole in the line of defense.

Me and Birdie miss daddy. I wish he could of been there so he could of seen me play football with all the skinny white boys. The ones who used to call me names and make fun of me for no reason, no reason at all except 'cause I was born a poor Mvskoke boy.

*haint – word was used by old-timers as a type of ghost

**TB – tuberculosis

Alan Elyshevitz

Alan Elyshevitz is the author of a collection of stories, *The Widows and Orphans Fund* (SFA Press), a full-length poetry collection, *Generous Peril* (Cyberwit), and five poetry chapbooks, most recently *Approximate Sonnets* (Orchard Street). Winner of the James Hearst Poetry Prize from *North American Review*, he is a two-time recipient of a fellowship in fiction writing from the Pennsylvania Council on the Arts.

ON RULES

Criminology

A quotable councilman with snow in his hair
demands that the public demand Teddy Roosevelt.
The commissioner claims that a handshake on the wrong
street corner is antisocial. A bailiff who eats breakfast
alone yearns to break opposable thumbs. The crime beat
wants to trammel more souls in a supermax. Studies show
that custody depends on a judge's eczema. One study shows
that the use of force is proportional to the academic
shortcomings of a policewoman's son. Another study shows
that leaving religious statuettes unattended increases
the arrest rate. A task force skims the budget of scholastic
nutrition, their report wrought with mercurial data,
according to which: Those who die of contaminants expire
in the throes of criminal minds. In the opinion of science,
the way to reduce the tragedy of public space is stasis.
Uninspire sudden movements by citizens, removing
every shadow of a shadow of a gun. On buses and libraries
hang banners that proclaim: Protect and serve yourself.

The Evolution of Labor

These days the workplace is less often a place of debacle
in cubicles during autumn's cancellations, where employees
don non-reflective attire and suffer leg cramps. Those days
of equivocation were days of transportation when the racket
of crankshafts in a tunnel underlied a river's lost momentum.
A memorandum on the virtues of cutting relieved cost
consciousness that looked good on paper with sleeves
rolled down. On desktops, muffin crumbs, a prelude to effort,
guided spreadsheets, those mental laxatives. My work now
proceeds in the ether with a network of theoretical strings.
Satellites swipe the atmosphere. I hear lamentations, hourly
check-ins, admonishments of software pings. My burnished
tax deductions rise in noontide glare. Joules strive for
the content of a jewel box, a perquisite achieved handsfree.

Alexis Ivy

Alexis Ivy is a 2018 recipient of the Massachusetts Cultural Council Fellowship in Poetry. She is the author of *Romance with Small-Time Crooks* (BlazeVOX [books], 2013) and *Taking the Homeless Census* (Saturnalia Books, 2020) which won the 2018 Saturnalia Editors Prize. She is co-editor of *Essential Voices: A COVID-19 Anthology* (West Virginia University Press, 2023). A recent resident of the Vermont Studio Center, she lives in her hometown Boston, working as an advocate for the homeless, and teaching in the PoemWorks community.

ON RULES

Instructions to All Persons:
erasure from Civilian Exclusion Order, 1947

alien and non-alien
are all that count

that intersection
limits the limits
                on a line
following to a point.
Beginning together

each individual,

alone

described as any person
entering
any act
as one
        alien
                be subject to
persons within
the bounds
of assembly.

Instruct order:
                enter.

McLeod's Plantation Speaks

Charleston, South Carolina

How much of my damaged history
can I claim?

Can I be historical context
and here-and-now context?

How do I preserve the past in the correct
way without complicity?

Am I here to change *legacy*
and *inheritance*?

What of my time so precious?
What of my world refurbished?

How can wrong be rightly shown
when trying to reckon with the past?

Should a place truly stay the same
when everything around it changes?

Am I still relevant?

The Bus Speaks

erasure from The Montgomery City Code, 1952

I
require
accommodations
for people

I
am in charge
firm operator

I
rat the race

I
am direction
for the purpose
of visions
any passenger
take a seat
belongs in a seat

I
carry passengers
any person
without excuse

Freedom Speaks

erasure from Security Handbook of Mississippi's Council of Federated
Organization

doors have locks
circling the day
circumstances attempt to tell reason
lock   up
at all times
all possession s
bizarre   provocative   prescribed
the facts will ask
the lives you remember your role in

I can go at all times full in and out
as much as possible
anywhere certain
at night absolutely
all unnecessary travel in and out of town
i circle
can be open windows
sleep
with the light
in front of the night

ON RULES

where you live you find
strangers to "look around"
bear in mind any time
information will be asked
take an interest in every person and
all times aware danger
i s white

We The People

> *"...and that the United States, if you can conceive it not so much as a place to be in but as an idea to believe in, it is worth fighting for."*
>
> –Clint Smith, *How the Word is Passed*

We the People includes

the man with crushed hands who showed me
which iceberg heads of lettuce were freshest
at the Star Market yesterday.

We the People pledge

to help the unhoused family-of-five,
but second guess if the john who overdosed
yesterday is eligible for the same help.

We the People have

the right to lie in mown grass
of public parks and get grass
in our hair from lying there.

We the People have

the right to keep the dirt
or wash our hands

ON RULES

in public water.

We the People serve

our country by explaining to
my father for the fifth time
what *she/they* means.

We the People witness

our waitress say *I thought you were white*
to my American boyfriend. I try to imagine someone
saying that to my white face with my white name.

We the People promise

to call ourselves
American whenever, wherever
we feel American.

Smita Das Jain

Smita Das Jain is a writer by passion and writes every day. Samples of her writing are visible in her home office, her sunny terrace garden, her husband's car, and the kitchen napkins. An author of two short story collections and a novel, Smita's short stories have found prominence in *Auroras and Blossoms, Twist and Twain, WriteFluence* and several other anthologies across the globe. She was the only Asian to be named in the Top 20 flash fiction winners list in the Spring 2022 contest of the prestigious *Women on Writing* (*WOW!*) magazine for women writers. A two-time TEDx speaker, Smita lives with her rockstar husband and adorable fourteen-year-old daughter in Gurugram, India.

ON RULES

Good Girls Be Damned

'Sshh. Don't laugh out loud. You are a girl,' Mom admonishes and glances around, mortified.

We are amidst a military event. Dad, a decorated Army Officer, is somewhere on the expansive ground, wielding the baton in the parade. Mom is seated among fellow Army wives in the third row of the erected stage, engrossed in discussions regarding the preparations for the forthcoming ladies' club meeting.

We, the children, have pressing matters of our own to discuss and are occupying the row behind our mothers. One of my friends imitates the principal of the sole school in the cantonment area where we all go, exaggerating her peculiar mannerisms and thick accent. All of us break into peals of laughter.

Truth be told, I don't understand what's so funny, but I join in the laughter so as not to be left out.

That's when Mom turns around and makes that remark.

It is my turn to feel embarrassed. Certainly, I was not the only one to laugh. And one doesn't care about the pitch of the laughter while laughing. *Why should one rein in happiness?*

Besides, my six-year-old self deems it unjust to be publicly scolded by my parents. *What will my friends think?* I look at the others, but they have moved on to different matters.

ON RULES

It is then I notice I am the lone girl in that row of lively children.

'Ma, why can't girls laugh out loud?' I inquire as she tucks me into bed later that night.

She looks at me in surprise, evidently taken off-guard. 'You ask too many questions,' she remarks. She always says that for any question I ask. I wonder why she does not directly answer them first.

'What's wrong with girls laughing loud?' I persist.

'People take notice,' she replies.

'So what, Ma?' I am puzzled. *What harm does it do if people notice children having a good time?*

'Good girls are supposed to be quiet without attracting attention.'

'Oh,' I murmur, processing this information. My school textbook doesn't mention this. 'But everyone in the group was laughing.'

'They were all boys. No one minds when they laugh. Your exuberance made you stand out in that group.'

'Why is it acceptable for boys to be noticed and not for girls?'

Mom rolls her eyes and rises from the bed. 'You will understand when you grow up. Those are enough questions for today, Missy. Good night.'

ON RULES

She switches off the light and departs, leaving me with more questions than answers. I shut my eyes and silently pray to God, hoping I don't have to wait long to grow up.

*

'No, don't do that,' I plead, but it's too late. The mischievous boy has taken a fancy to the colorful spine of a book placed precisely in the middle of a tall pile and makes a beeline for it. The entire stack stumbles like a house of cards, creating chaos on the floor to my left.

'See what you have done,' I fume, surveying the fallen pile. I didn't want Parth in my room in the first place. I am exasperated. A critical ninth-grade exam looms tomorrow, and my father's colleague has chosen this day to visit our home with his family. His elder son is secluded in my brother's room, while the younger one wanders aimlessly amidst the adults settling down to pints of beer and animated conversation. Struggling to concentrate on my book amid the din, I now find myself compelled to clean up the mess.

The resounding crash draws the attention of our mothers to the room. Excellent, I thought. *Parth deserves some reprimand.* 'This is no way to talk to a young guest, Mita,' Mom says, taking me by surprise. 'Please say sorry to Parth.'

I want to shout, scream and laugh at the same time. 'What have I done, Ma?' I ask instead, attempting to comprehend my mother's statement. It was the young Parth who had caused the disturbance.

'You shouldn't have raised your voice. Parth is our guest,' Mom says.

ON RULES

'Let it go, Soma. Parth is fine.' Parth's mother tries to placate mine. Of course, Parth is fine. *What could be amiss with him?*

'No. Mita needs to learn some manners. Shouting and screaming are not appropriate.'

I regard myself as a well-mannered girl who occasionally raises her voice when required. My brother, four years my senior, is generally much louder than I am.

'But Ma, brother talks loudly all the time. And in this instance, it was Parth who was distracting me from my studies.' I hadn't even shouted then. The disorder in my room led me to lose my composure. I don't believe I should be held accountable for that.

'Girls don't shout, Mita. At least good girls don't.'

I gaze at her in dismay. I am good at studies, thrive in extracurricular activities, and consistently obey my parents. *Doesn't all of that qualify me as a good girl?*

'Now, say sorry to Parth and then tidy up the room. You can get back to your studies later,' my mother persists.

'I will not say sorry to anyone,' I burst into tears and dash out of the room into my father's arms. I am not going to apologize when someone else is at fault. Good girls be damned.

*

'You cannot join the Army,' Mom declares, her words carrying an air of incredulity that seems more wistful than authoritative. Over the years, I've evolved into a rebel who prefers charting her own course based on her heart's compass rather than adhering to others' directives.

'You never objected when brother made a similar decision,' I counter, fully aware of her anticipated response.

'It's different for him. He is a boy. The armed forces aren't a place for women.'

'Only you believe so, Ma. The government disagrees. There must be a reason for it to sanction permanent commission for women in the armed forces.' The significant announcement earlier in the year felt tailored to fit my aspirations. Since the age of five, I've harbored dreams of donning the olive-green uniform adorned with stars on the shoulder blades. Nothing and no one could come between me and my dream, not even myself.

'Girls don't join the army,' she repeats, turning to my father. 'Please drill some sense into your daughter,' she implores, seeking support. Dad glances at me. My heart sinks, palms shake and lips quiver. I remain his little girl. No matter what's at stake, I won't be able to defy him.

'Army life is demanding, Mita,' he says. It's a statement he needn't make. I've witnessed it firsthand over my eighteen years of existence. I craved more of my father, but duty often kept him in far-flung locations where family couldn't accompany him. Although his seniority has eased the situation, the memories persist.

I meet his gaze and pose the question, 'Can you envision yourself anywhere other than the armed forces?'

ON RULES

He returns my steady look. 'No,' he confesses. 'Can you?' I vigorously shake my head. 'Are you certain about this, Mita?' he asks, adopting the gentle tone that fathers reserve for their daughters. 'I am,' I affirm.

'Alright, then. You may join the military academy. I hope to witness you as part of the inaugural group of permanently commissioned women officers in the forces, so ensure you successfully navigate the rigorous training.'

I can't believe my ears. *Why does this surprise me*? I can't recall a single instance where my father has denied my wishes.

'Yipeee!' I exclaim, rushing towards him. 'Thank you,' I express, enveloping him in a heartfelt hug.

'What is this?' An incredulous voice emanates from our right. 'You are allowing her to follow her whims,' Mom interjects.

'Who are we to permit her or deny her, Soma?' Dad rationalizes. 'She is an adult capable of making her own decisions.'

'She's also a girl and needs to learn to heed others. It will be challenging otherwise.'

Why should I succumb to gender expectations imposed by others? The question crosses my mind, but I am too elated to voice it. For once, I am able to pursue *my* desires.

*

ON RULES

'What are you doing in the ring? You are a woman.' I shrug off the words, assuming my fighting stance. These words, once left behind at home, have become a daily encounter in the academy.

This world is no different from the one back home. It is a man's world. As a woman, I have to fight every day to assert my presence.

There are only five women in the batch of one hundred and fifty cadets. The government's decision to grant permanent commissions to women hasn't translated into infrastructure upgrades. There is no separate changing room for women, for instance.

But more than the infrastructure, the mindset needs to change.

The banter at the dinner table halts when I take my place. While there's eagerness among men to partner with the five women for dance at parties, the same men avoid choosing women as combat training partners. As a result, women often partner with each other, leaving one of us as the odd one out. The staff at the academy, accustomed to default salutes for 'sirs,' struggle with 'ma'am' and hesitate to accord us the same honor. Instructors – battle-hardened army men – with kid gloves, reluctant to assign us hardcore physical activities.

At every step, with each passing day, I am made to feel I do not belong here. And that's unacceptable to me. I had cleared the entrance exam on my dint, cleared the grueling physical rounds with ease, and was at the institute on merit. I deserve my place here. Yet, I seem to be the lone believer in my worth at the academy.

Taking matters into my own hands, I decide to be the first woman to enter the academy's boxing championships.

ON RULES

'I can't fight you,' the fellow officer continues.

'Scared?' I taunt. 'You can concede the match. I won't come after you.'

My words have the intended effect. My opponent enters the ring, removes his robe and gets into position. His pale blue attire contrasts sharply with my vibrant red. He doesn't want to lose face in front of his peers, and I don't want to think of my face while packing punches. It's the same arena, but we have different motives to fight.

The white-clad referee in the middle of the ring blows a black whistle, signaling the beginning of the bout.

For the next thirty minutes, I pour everything into the fight – pulling, punching, shoving, and diving. Uncertain where to strike, my opponent hesitates, and I exploit this tentativeness. The fear of becoming a laughingstock in the institute's history breaks his inhibitions, and he starts throwing punches at me. We engage in a fierce battle.

I move to deflect his blow, which lands very hard on my jaw. *Crunch.* The sound reverberates in the packed but hushed room. *Did something break?*

'There's blood on her face,' my opponent screams in a hysterical manner. He stops.

'Come on, let's fight,' I attempt to say. Only garbled sounds escape my mouth.

'Take Mita to the hospital. Now,' someone commands from the back. The world around me starts to fade. I can't let this happen. I need to win the fight. 'I will finish the match,' I insist.

ON RULES

'Match over,' the referee calls, exhibiting a red card to my opponent. He has been disqualified. A watershed moment unfolds in the military academy's century-old legacy as a female participates in and triumphs in a boxing match. I have etched my name in history.

Too drained to savor my triumph, I collapse into my opponent's arms.

Regaining consciousness, I find myself in a hospital room. My jaw bears the weight of various supports, and a cannula restricts my left wrist. Turning my gaze, I see my erstwhile opponent standing by my bedside, with concern evident on his face.

'How are you feeling?' he inquires.

As I attempt to respond, pain radiates from my mouth to my head. I squeeze my eyes, halting the tears.

'You will be fine,' he reassures. 'Don't say anything.'

A nurse enters just then, inserting a syringe into my free arm. 'Ouch,' I yell. Injections invariably hurt.

'You are a woman. Learn to endure the pain,' the female nurse remarks. The casual comment doesn't sit well with me.

'Indeed, I am a woman. That doesn't mean I can't feel and express my pain,' I assert. The discomfort on my face pales compared to the anguish in my heart. At home, it was my mother; here it is this nurse. *Why do women make it more difficult for other women to progress?*

ON RULES

My words devolve into unintelligible sounds. 'Easy, Mita,' the fellow officer consoles. 'It will be fine soon.'

I sigh and close my eyes. *How can it be fine till women secure equal rights?* I don't expect a man to understand when women themselves haven't.

*

'I don't want to marry. How often must I reiterate my stance for it to register with you?'

'For how long will you remain single? You are twenty-six,' my mother remarks, as though I've surpassed a half-century milestone. Society deems me too old for the marriage market and, apparently, too formidable to handle. 'Few are willing to consider a working woman, let alone an Army Major, as a prospective bride,' she continues.

'And I deem them unworthy of me,' I counter. 'Why should I marry someone when I am not interested?'

'All women marry,' my mother insists.

'Some marry by choice, while others succumb to the relentless pressure exerted upon them.' Mom raises an eyebrow and rolls her eyes – an expression of disapproval to which I've grown accustomed.

'I don't want to marry. I want to be happy,' I persist.

'Who says you can't be happy after marriage?'

ON RULES

'I have yet to encounter a friend who's happy after getting hitched.'

'You must have the wrong friends, then. Look at me. I am happy.'

I refrain from pointing out that despite having a gentleman like my father as her spouse, Mom always appeared busy, preoccupied, and fatigued. With the head of the household stationed in remote border areas for half their thirty-five years of married life, she raised two children and managed an expansive home on her own.

Yet, instead of acknowledging this, I inadvertently hit below the belt to strengthen my argument. 'You are a housewife, Ma. You don't comprehend the challenges of balancing work and family. It was easier for you to be happy.'

The words hang in the air, sounding harsh as soon as they leave my mouth. Regrettably, there's no way I can take them back. Mom gapes, shadows darkening her eyes. I've tested her patience countless times, but this is the first time I've seen her genuinely hurt.

'So, you believe managing a home is challenging only if you earn money on the side? That overseeing household affairs and caring for two lively children is a mere cakewalk,' she retorts, wounded by my careless words.

'Sorry, Ma. That was thoughtless of me,' I interject, though in vain, as she presses on. 'You think it was easy for me to relinquish my career after marriage?'

'No, not at all. But consider, you had to sacrifice your career due to marriage and the ensuing responsibilities, right?' I attempt to reason, clutching at the straw of an opening she's provided. 'I don't want to go through that.'

ON RULES

'I gave up my career because I loved your brother the moment he was born and couldn't fathom leaving him at a childcare facility or with a nanny. The same holds true for you. But how can someone who only values money understand the depth of love?'

'Hey, that's unfair. I don't only value money. I value my independence. I don't want to compromise it through marriage just because society expects it.'

'Then introduce me to the person you love, and we will arrange your marriage.'

'I have not fallen in love with anyone.'

'So, there's no love marriage on the anvil. You are adamant against arranged marriage. What do you plan to do? Live out your old age in solitude?'

'People pass away alone – whether old or young. Their loved ones don't accompany them.'

'At least think of your brother. We are delaying his marriage because of yours.'

I sit upright, surprised by this revelation. 'But why? If he's ready, why wait for me?'

'What will people say? A marriageable girl stays at home while her younger brother gets married. No, girls should marry first.'

'It's high time girls pursue what they want. I don't want to get married. At least not now. You can decide whether you want my brother to surpass marriageable age while waiting for me to change my mind,' I said, returning to the book I was reading.

ON RULES

Mom lingers for some time but eventually retreats upon seeing me resolutely immersed in my world.

I know she's disappointed. But I can't help it. I've resolved not to conform to expectations, even if those expectations come from my loved ones.

*

'What do we do? He… I mean, she is a woman.' The towering, masked gunman queries the second one. It appears to be an unprecedented situation for him. It was an unusual circumstance for me as well.

My regiment is posted in *Kupwara* in *Jammu and Kashmir,* a densely forested area prone to frequent infiltration by insurgents from across the border. As the second-in-command of my battalion, I relish being on the front lines of the regular skirmishes between the Army and these non-state actors.

The incident in the last twenty-four hours was a full-scale battle, not a skirmish. Five masked militants surrounded a military convoy en route to our base for replacements and threw a grenade at the party. When the dust settled, there were five lifeless bodies.

The militants escaped into the adjoining dense forest. Shortly after, a combat team of fourteen from my regiment engaged in a gun battle with them. I, the only woman on the squad, was leading them.

It was a fierce encounter amidst the shrubs and shadows. Those five seemed to know every nook and cranny of the forest as if it were their home while we had to find our own way. Nevertheless, my men managed to shoot two of them dead after eight hours. Three of them were still at large. My team and I weren't going to give up until we neutralized all the miscreants.

Night fell, and I contemplated pausing the operation and reevaluating the next day's strategy. That's when a swift rustle reached my ears. I followed the sound without a second thought. I should have.

Before I could realize it, the futile pursuit took me a long way away from the rest of my team. I was lost amid the thick vegetation, with no human in sight. Suddenly, the plantation gave way to an open ground, and I caught my breath as my eyes dazzled at the sight of the twinkling stars in the clear sky. That's when two men ambushed me from behind, gagged and masked me, tied my hands, and transported me to another corner of the dense land.

It wasn't until they halted and peeled the mask from my face, they discovered I was a woman.

'Afraid of a woman, are you?' I taunt them, notwithstanding my plight. That's the only way I can think of extricating myself from this perilous situation.

They cast a surprised gaze my way before the shorter one sneers, 'You have some cheek. Can you imagine what we can do with you in this forest? Your men will take ages to locate you. By the time we are through with you, you will rue why you are still alive.'

'You aren't married, are you?' The taller one inquires. 'Today, we will familiarize you with the sensations of carnal pleasure.'

ON RULES

A shiver of fear, anger, and disgust courses through my spine, but I force myself to stay silent. Shouting would only play into their hands.

'I would relish that,' I say sweetly. 'Why don't you summon your third partner, too, and we can take turns?' Even in the dark, I discern the bewildered expressions on their faces.

'If something is inevitable, might as well go ahead and enjoy it. Resistance won't yield any results, so I might as well savor the pleasures of the body,' I persist in goading them.

The taller one steps forward. 'You are playing games with us.'

'I am telling you a fact. It's entirely up to you if you don't wish to take advantage of me. The long day must have gotten to you. I understand. Not everyone can be man enough.'

'What are you saying?' My abductor bristles. 'Of course, I am a man.'

'Prove it then. Let me feel your manliness with my bare hands.'

With a feverish urgency, he unties my hands. 'No,' the other one cries on deaf ears. I lunge forward and embrace him tightly once my hands are free. I can feel the desire emanating from him as he enfolds me in his arms.

We resemble ardent lovers beneath the starry night.

'You smell great,' he says.

'I also kill great,' I whisper. *Plunk*. The long and thin knife I had hidden in my sleeve pierces his chest before he can release me from his embrace.

ON RULES

He recoils, letting go of me, staring at the knife in shock. In a swift motion, I extract the blade from his body. The cry of agony reverberates through the forest. There's no way it will escape the ears of my colleagues.

The insurgent drops to his knees on the ground, the shock on his face surpassing the convulsions of his body. He will soon be dead.

I hear the second one shout obscenities as he rushes towards me. Balancing my weight swiftly on one leg, I deliver a precise strike to his shin with the other, denying him the chance to complete his sentence. Without a moment's hesitation, I thrust the knife blade deeply through his abdomen, twisting the blade. The steel emerges on the opposite side, now adorned in a deep shade of red, an indistinguishable blend of both men's blood.

As he crumples to the ground in death, I mutter, 'May you be reborn as women in your next life.'

I am sorting through their pockets for phones and identification when my team arrives. Relief washes over me as I notice the third militant in their custody.

'Thank goodness you're safe. We were worried,' one of them expresses.

'Not because I am a woman, I hope,' I quip. The remark catches the poor fellow off guard. His gaze shifts from me to the fallen culprits, then back to me.

'How did you manage to neutralize both of them?' I sense admiration in his tone.

'I exploited their vulnerability for the flesh,' I reply after a pause. 'After all, I am a woman.'

ON RULES

*

'I am honored to present this distinguished gallantry award to an esteemed woman officer,' declares the President of the Nation.

This momentous occasion unfolds on Republic Day. I've spent my formative years witnessing the grand display of the country's military might near the *India Gate, New Delhi*, each year. My father, a three-time leader of his unit in the Republic Day march, now sits among the five thousand-strong audience, a spectator alongside my mother.

Leading my contingent in the Republic Day parade was a dream I never dared to harbor. The notion of receiving one of the country's highest gallantry medals on this illustrious day was beyond the scope of my imagination.

But dreams materialize even if you don't dream them.

'In her two-year tenure in Kashmir, Mita led her unit with unwavering courage through fifteen counter-insurgent operations, neutralizing twenty-two terrorists in the process,' resonates the announcer, introducing me to the crowd.

I steal a glance at the front-row spectators on the far right, where I stand in anticipation. *Is it a trick of the mind, or is my father wiping tears from his eyes?*

As the nation's leader commends me while bestowing the medal on my chest and neatly folded citation in my hand, I stand as the sole woman among the fifteen honored.

'Honorable Sir,' I address, my voice quivering and my legs betraying a subtle tremor, 'I am an officer who happens to be a woman. The day we transcend gender barriers and acknowledge recognition solely on the grounds of merit, the day when accommodations for women become redundant as they are already proportionately represented, the day when countless more Mitas are recognized in the Republic Day ceremony – that will be the day when women will genuinely arrive. I hope I live to see that day.'

The President maintains a stoic expression. *Is this his usual demeanor, or have I offended him?* My heart races, and beads of sweat trickle down my forehead. *Have I said too much?*

Then, a warm smile breaks across his face as he pats my shoulders. 'Well said,' he compliments. 'I'll discuss this with the Prime Minister and explore what can be done. I genuinely wish for you to enjoy a long and healthy life and pray you don't have to wait long for that transformative day.'

I offer a smart salute, turn around, and march forward. Though my head is held high, I struggle to contain the tears that threaten to spill from my eyes.

It is ok for girls to cry, they say. It may be, but I am determined not to conform to societal stereotypes and norms – at least not in public.

*

'Are you sure you want to do this?' Mom inquires.

I am on a week's leave and spending quality time with my parents. My mind is preoccupied after revealing my decision to them.

ON RULES

I have resolved to embrace motherhood. I remain equally steadfast about not getting married. My intention is to initiate the adoption process to nurture a girl child.

'Haven't been sure of anything more in my life,' I affirm.

'That's quite a statement,' Mom chuckles. 'You have always been headstrong, unyielding in the pursuit of what you desire.'

'What are you saying?' I playfully protest, pleasantly taken aback by her lack of uproar or discouragement.

'You'll need to figure out how to take care of her during your field postings,' Dad interjects. 'Raising a child single-handedly is no mean feat.'

Mom steps in before I can respond. 'I'm confident our daughter has considered everything. Besides, what are we here for? I'll offer my assistance whenever she needs it.'

'Thank you so much, Ma,' I muster, grateful for this strong support from an unexpected quarter.

Mom squeezes my hands. 'Will you promise me one thing?' she asks.

I look at her. *What can she want?* 'Don't raise her like I raised you, enforcing different sets of rules for boys and girls. Instead, be the mother I wasn't, showing her she can achieve anything she wants. Tell her there are no gender roles and rules.'

ON RULES

I don't attempt to hold back the free-flowing tears from my eyes as I tighten my grip on her hands. Though unaccustomed to shedding tears, my mother's words have struck a chord deep in my heart.

It is acceptable to cry. For anyone. As Mom mentioned, there are no gender roles and rules. When humanity embraces and practices this belief, the world will be inherently more egalitarian.

Natalie Jill

Natalie Jill's most recent work has appeared or is upcoming in *Free State Review, Atlanta Review, Sugar House Review,* and *Unleash Lit*. She is a member of the PoemWorks community in the Boston area.

ON RULES

Dissociating in Clinical Seminar

I'm learning in school
that you aren't
supposed to touch me.

> My dissociation is a pilgrimage
> to the International Space Station.

You aren't supposed to
place your hand
on top of my head.

> A couple miles off the earth,
> the crowding thins.
>   Just a stray butterfly, some
> birds, an escaped balloon,
> those puffy cumulus.

You aren't supposed to
run your knuckle
down my cheek.

> Far past the ozone
> that's healing nicely,
> the blue sky darkens.

ON RULES

You aren't supposed to
squeeze my toes when they
come near you

> This trek seems shorter
> than El Camino de Santiago,
> with only a passing satellite.

on the couch we share,
out from under the
blanket you wrapped me in.

> Once onboard, the crew
> brings me straight to
> the window, shows me
> the astonishment of color,

I'm worried you aren't
supposed to love me this way.
I'm worried you'll stop.

> every season strung
> beneath a blue line,
> the curvature of the world.

ON RULES

About belonging

My Mom had just told me I could only bring
one stuffed animal on vacation.
They were all at the end
of the bed, smiling at me, loving me,

wanting to be with me. I sobbed.
When I'm gone, the others will cry.
They'll rub their own arms, aching and hollow.
They'll grasp the blankets. They'll be unchosen.

I looked up at the kindly face
of my tiger, who I was about to abandon,
and something broke through:
his feelings are up to me.

It turned out, I decided, that he didn't even
want to come with me after all.
None of them did, except one: my teddy,
oldest, with matted fur. The rest all asked,

together, to stay behind on the bed.
All huddled and content,
just fine without me.
I wish they wanted me to stay.

ON RULES

Vantage

When I'm lying on
that baseball field in
the dark, Pendleton under
me, thermos of tea
somewhere in reach
of my right arm, staring
at the stars,

at this latitude
I'm actually plastered
nearly upright. "Up" is
what we call going
against gravity.
What we call "up"
is actually "out."

The world turns
a thousand miles
per hour, and I'm
looking out beyond
what holds me
to its surface,
beyond the over-

whelming pull,

ON RULES

somewhere
directionless,
where everything
is both easy
and, therefore,
impossible.

Halyna Koba

Amidst the busyness of life, Halyna Koba, who lives in Hamilton, Ontario, Canada, has always identified herself as a writer. She holds an Honours B.A., majoring in Journalism from the University of Western Ontario. Now a content retiree, she writes poetry, walks, reads, plays Texas Hold 'Em Poker, and participates in poetry workshops (Tower Poetry Society) and poetry slams (Hamilton You Poets).

ON RULES

Doing My Own Thing

i eat mac and cheese

with a spoon when i'm alone,

and no one is hurt

Sharon E. Ludan

Sharon E. Ludan holds a B.A. from the College of New Jersey and an M.S. from Boston University. As an American diplomat, Ludan has lived and worked in many countries throughout the world. Her work has been published by Proverse Hong Kong, Wingless Dreamer, Quillkeepers Press, Unleash Press; the Kansai Scene; the OSIPP Journal, and elsewhere.

ON RULES

The Elasticity of Time

You may stretch it or
bend it; use, lose
or spend it; save it or
waste it, make it or
break it.

Time may whiz or drag by;
drip, flash or fly; you

cannot suspend it, undo
or rewind it.

Don't
try to stop it, freeze it or
block it.

(You never know
how much time you're allotted!)

You may have too little
or much on your hands;
others may ask you to spare them a bit.

(In fact it may make the very best gift.)

ON RULES

Some claim you can buy it –
but at what price?

You can't really own it, can
have but not hold it.

(Oddly, the rich often lack it the most.)

Time's a manmade invention,
a curious confection.

We measure and count
and regulate time:

days, hours and minutes,
time zones and epochs,
decades, centuries,
eons and eras.

You may divide your time
in calendar slots; set alarms,
bells and whistles
on your phone or watch.

Truth is said to be ageless,
wisdom ripens with time;
but beauty and vigor perversely decline.

ON RULES

Einstein believed
time's inseparable from space --
a fourth dimension
in spacetime continuum.

And everyone has a distinct
worldline
in the greater fabric of all spacetime.

Our worldlines may sync
for a short or long while;

we're here and
we're there; we come and
we go;

we're always
and everywhere
part of the whole.

We may never unravel time's
cosmic enigma,
may not control our beginning or end.

But we can each
seize this chance

ON RULES

of a whole lifetime

to create and
fulfill
our unique worldline.

ON RULES

Advance Confidently

Tell me, what is it you plan to do
with your one wild and precious life?

—Mary Oliver, "The Summer Day"

Sometimes I think
death is a ploy

to prod us to live our best lives.

We don't know how long we have,
or even why.

There may be rules; or
maybe you make your own.

And anyway,
what's the whole point?

You might as well do what you want –
right now!
while you have time.

But do what,
precisely?

ON RULES

Some lucky ones
know their what from the get-go:
a precocious talent, or
irresistible proclivity.

Others may have
a eureka moment, or
fortuitous encounter with their destiny.

Some
cast about aimlessly,
wandering down lanes of
least resistance.

Or someone may come along
and pull you in their direction; that
may be fun for a while, but...

Advance confidently
suggests Thoreau.

Just choose a direction, any direction you like;
give it your all.

If it doesn't work, adjust course;
repeat as needed.

ON RULES

In the end,
we all arrive at the same destination,
no matter which path you take.

Furthermore,
maybe there is no
one right direction, no
singular destiny to be discovered.

Perhaps it's *all* right, including
the false starts, wrong turns,
dead ends, and yes, even
the egregious mistakes...

Maybe life truly is
what you make it;

not only the what but
the *how* of it.

Every encounter, every
experience
sinks into your being,

becomes who you are -- the unique
who of you.

ON RULES

So go ahead -- be bold,
advance confidently.

Life may surprise you yet.

Nick Manning

Nick Manning is a British man in his early 70s, living happily with his husband, dog and, sometimes, stepson in Washington DC and New York. He cycles determinedly but uneasily in both neighborhoods. He retired from the World Bank some years ago and is the author of a large number of distinctly dry technical books and papers about governments and their dysfunctions, an output of which kept him busy for most of his career.

ON RULES

Rules of the Road: A Fable

1.   When the old rules ruled

Mary and Peter were friends and neighbors. They lived liberal, peaceful, single, white lives with Saturday morning coffees and good-natured trades in the convertible currencies of child and dog minding. They each pretended to care about a different local basketball team and would joke-mock the other when 'their' team lost. They often talked about ending their respective spouselessnesses, risking their reputations and maybe their lives by trying internet dating. They both denied the reality of an inchoate and menacing world. Their awareness that Iran would gain nuclear weapons and that the polar ice caps would completely melt in their lifetimes did not cause the panic that these insights merited as they both thought that the universe's many and various moral, technological and communal arcs all bend towards justice and other similar good things. After all, their parents had seen progress in the struggle for civil rights, they could see a growing cohort of rechargeable Prius sedans and Wholefoods had started selling Palestinian olive oil.

The topologies of Peter and Mary's lots were exactly the same. Both yards sloped down away from the house towards the same alley. There was just enough of an angle to encourage errant balls to roll and take their place in the quasi-hedge of tall weeds that grew at the bottom of the yards under the unsightly chain link fence that both properties relied on to prevent alley-goers from trespassing.

The contents of their gardens were not identical but, Twain-like, they rhymed. Mary's garden had metal chairs, a little the worse for wear but refreshed by the new cushions which Amazon had recently delivered. The chairs stood, with a corresponding table, on a brick patio outside her kitchen. The other half of her yard was grass, damaged by the determined efforts of her kids and dissected by a concrete path leading pointlessly to the nasty chain link fence that ran along the back. Peter's yard had a wooden table and bench, allegedly mahogany but since it was falling to pieces that seemed questionable, placed on a small concrete patio outside of his kitchen. The remainder of his yard was also grass, dissected by an equally unnecessary path and damaged by the biochemical action of his lazy Jack Russel's toilet habits. His path was made from bricks very similar to those underneath Mary's metal chairs. The concrete of her path, with its widening cracks and ever-eager algae, was of the same stuff as his patio.

So, the back gardens of their adjoining houses matched. Peter and Mary speculated that the equality in sizes and the mirroring in shapes had been determined by waistcoated city planners who marked out the lots before selling what was then unpromising marshland to hungry nineteenth century developers. They would joke that the planners were probably sepia-toned in real life.

They were looking, from their respective sides, at the wooden fence which divided the matching back gardens. The seasons had converted the wooden panels into brittle gray material showing that biodegradation was winning its long struggle against the preservatives injected into the timber. The fence had a hole through which Mary's children and Peter's lazy Jack Russell could wriggle.

"As a rule, good fences make good neighbors," Peter said.

"I had a wild thought," Mary replied. "What if we broke the rule and took it down? Kids and canine would all enjoy the bigger space."

It's probable that each party felt that they would get the better of this deal. Mary might have calculated that allowing the canine toilet damage to extend to her side would be a small price to pay for a larger play area for the kids. And maybe Peter had long nurtured the idea of bricking over his patio or concreting over hers to create a large and glorious shared space. He might well have also hoped that this would lead to his only paying half the cost of a large and glorious new patio set.

Peter's logical observation that "we'd have to put something up again if one of us ever sold our house" undoubtedly frightened Mary as it carried an implication that he foresaw this as a possibility. After all, widowed and no family, he could sell up and spend everything, calibrating the expenditure on his nursing care, precision-timing his passing of the responsibility to Medicare ensuring that he would have minimal time sharing a room in a care home with a geriatric stranger and that his savings would just hit zero at his death. She had a long-gone, contribute-nothing ex-husband and her kids cost a surprising amount to run. It would take more guts than she had to plan on leaving them nothing and the house was the thing that she had to leave to them. So, she was doomed to stay there until the end and it would have been disconcerting to be reminded that he had other options.

Nevertheless, the idea grew and ripened in the late summer, reaching maturity just as Mary's 'regular house guy' came to fix the gutter.

"Shall we do it – we can ask Jose and split the costs?" she suggested perkily.

"One delightful bit of absurdity," Peter told her, "is that we're removing the only physical evidence of the boundary between the Advisory Neighborhood Commission districts." They had both become marginally familiar with the arcane workings of these Washington DC entities when they protested the proposal to build a new apartment block on a vacant lot near the local church, long used by local children as a safe place to mess around on their bikes. Cars were at the center of their stated concerns. Peter said that he was worried that the underground car park for the new block would not be big enough, leading to yet more people parking where they should not. For her, more residents meant more cars, more emissions and, very particularly, more dangerously irritated and impatient driving. The common theme of drivers and their propensity to break parking and speeding rules made their objections rhyme like their back gardens. She wanted safety with an aroma of environmentalism. He wanted parking and the feel of a small town.

Membership of the ANC was based on hyper-local elections. 'Commissioners' were elected from tiny constituencies based on seemingly random boundaries containing a couple of hundred households. The meeting to decide the ANC's position on the proposed new building had been held at a church hall where a map, layered with public transport routes, buried power cables, sewer lines, and administrative boundaries, was pinned up on the wall. That was when Peter and Mary saw that the boundary between Commissioners' constituencies followed a vaguely logical line up the center of the larger street to the west of their homes but then jerked down their street to go between their houses and backyards before veering back to its original course.

2. The uneven rise of uneven rules

New bike lanes were bringing in novel and asymmetric rules. Cars were forbidden to drive or park in the newly painted lanes, while cyclists were allowed to ride wherever they wanted. Mary liked the general tipping of the balance in favor of the cyclists but felt that her concerns about the risks to cyclists, including her kids, from poor driving had still not been adequately addressed.

ON RULES

"You just can't trust drivers to follow the rules and a white line painted on the road is not exactly a car-proof barrier," she said to Peter one Saturday morning in early summer as they sat around their shared patio table on their jointly owned reclining patio chairs under their new and elaborate cantilever patio umbrella. Mary's kids were a little older now, but she still worried about them cycling on the roads, even with the newly painted lanes.

"I don't see why we need any of this," Peter responded. "If we just all obeyed the existing rules of the road then we'd all be fine. Anyway, city roads weren't built for bikes."

"Well the roads weren't built for cars either," Mary responded with unusual sharpness. "When these places were built, you got around in a horse and carriage. By the way, did you see the leaflet about a protected bike lane?"

He hadn't – either it had been thrown away or he had been spared. She fetched one and showed him that there was a plan to create a dedicated lane for bikes on the larger street to the west. It would be 'protected,' ingeniously, by moving the cars parked along the western side of the street about four feet away from the sidewalk, creating a corridor in which a row of parked cars would serve as a barrier between car and bike lanes. It was coming up to ANC election time and the leaflet was from a candidate for her district's Commissioner position – a candidate who thought that protected bike lanes in general, PBLs as he called them as if they were the next stage in the evolution of children's sandwiches, were terrible ideas.

"Oh – it's an ANC election pamphlet," Peter said. "That's why I didn't get one. I'm in a different ANC district."

ON RULES

"I support the plan," she said. "That's a bike lane that I'd let the kids use. Drivers can't be trusted to follow the rules and this means that cyclists are still safe."

"I read about these PBLs. There are several problems," Peter noted, rather primly. "Fewer parking places and narrower roads, so more congestion. And seniors and disabled people have to cross a bike super-highway when they go to the stores. And we're going to see all these Lycra-wearing youngsters racing through our neighborhood. And then there's the bloody scooters."

"Why's the tidal wave of Lycra a problem?" Mary asked, somewhat arbitrarily picking on the penultimate concern.

"It's just more crowding, more density, more urban hipsters who don't live here, zooming through on their way to the latest cold brew coffee shop."

They laughed about their differing policy positions. A few days later, they laughed again as they each confessed that they would be running for the Commissioner positions in their neighboring ANC districts.

"It will be fun. It's great – we can just let the debate play out and see where things end up. I'm in favor of the PBLs – you're not. But if we get a protected bike lane or we don't, it's not, like, a huge issue."

Peter was the only candidate for his district, running on a verbose platform of 'no more highway engineering – just follow the rules and share the streets.' Mary circulated her photocopied campaign slogan, 'cars and bikes – separate but equal,' to all the households in her district. She was up against an anti-PBL candidate but he dropped out, concussed by a speeding cyclist it was rumored.

ON RULES

They were each elected to their respective ANC districts, her doubts about the rule compliance of drivers and her support for PBLs rhyming nicely with his conviction that the rules of adhering to speed limits and trying not to injure anyone were quite adequate.

They walked together to and from the ANC meetings and sat together on their joint patio laughing at the seriousness with which their fellow Commissioners treated the outraged concerns of neighbors about unrepaired streetlights.

The fun faded as motions were proposed in favor of extending the protected bike lane, widening the protected bike lane to make it two way, and adding *more* protection to the protected bike lane with elaborate thickets of plastic bollards. Those supporting the motions provided PowerPoint decks that began with a two-slide opening prayer to the gods of multi-modal long-range transportation planning and Department of Transport performance objectives. The presentations focused on process, outlining the laudable way the city works with regional and federal partners such as the National Parks Service, and the intricacy of the arrangements for assessing commercial loading and ADA-compliant parking needs. The city's PowerPoint presentation announced, with an implicit fanfare, that a further ten miles of protected bike lane would be constructed before the end of that financial year. An asterisk on the last slide in the city's slide deck referred any eagle-eyed readers to a tiny comment at the bottom noting that there would be some minor loss of parking spaces.

Those arguing against PBLs had passion but no PowerPoints. They were from churches who feared the loss of parking spaces that became so important every Sunday morning, from activists for disabled people who took the opportunity to reprimand all present for ignoring their existence, and from self-proclaimed defenders of the community who were sure that local merchants would face bankruptcy when customers could no longer pull up directly in front of their stores. In sharp contrast to the steady tones of the motion proposers, the opponents had the distinctive vocal wobbles that always arise when fear of public speaking meets the certainty of a cause. They told stories of local residents, of elderly and disabled people, of parents with small children, of heavily pregnant women, all left searching for parking spaces blocks and blocks away from their homes or forced to unload groceries from the back of an Uber before facing an onslaught of cyclists silently speeding between them and their front doors. They suggested that all these innocent victims of the bike lane obsession were being forced into death marches, exposed to the increasing numbers of assaults and shootings which this city government had left unaddressed as it put its energy into this unnecessary war on cars. And all that cyclists and drivers had to do was to follow the rules – and then the PBLs would not be needed.

Mary voted in favor of the motion supporting the construction of a protected bike lane on the larger street to the west of their properties. Peter voted against, arguing that trust in sensible driving was more sustainable than plastic bollards. If they harbored anger or even a smidge of irritation towards the other, then none of this was visible. However it was now impossible for them to walk to or from the ANC meetings together because their respective pro- and anti-PBL caucuses had conflicting timetables. It was winter and so there was no opportunity to use their shared patio.

3.   The old rules have gone

NEXTDOOR

Truth Pedaler's post is trending: *Private cars must be banned within our municipal boundaries. Scooters, bikes, electric taxis, and buses must be*

ON RULES

unleashed. Death is a small price to pay if it awakens us. Death is the only thing that will give the city life.

Mary's skepticism about the willingness of drivers to adhere to the rules of the road delayed her recognition that cyclists and scooter users were increasingly anarchic, prone to downgrading red stop lights to merely an advisory role. They based this on the assumption that their vulnerability and environmental credentials shielded them from both criticism and danger. For the increasingly angry drivers, these non-conforming cyclists and scooter users had become a category unto themselves, a homogenous mass, a subspecies they could comfortably despise. Drivers' heart-stopping panic upon realizing this was the night they nearly triggered weeks of insurance paperwork was now counterbalanced by the thrill that a cyclist cutting in front of them while dressed entirely in black on a bike with no lights might get their just, if fatal, desserts. Mary had long noted the hypocrisy of car drivers who raced along narrow streets while texting, outraged by the cyclists whose misbehavior was much less dangerous than their own, but she started to gain some insight that virtue was not one sided. She did not mention this to Peter, and he certainly did not share any nascent thoughts that perhaps some motorists were irredeemable.

As cyclists saw less reason to follow any rules, they relied on the protection of their personal deities, big or little gods that rewarded them for their environmental efforts and judged car drivers for their carbon emissions. These gods of carbon-free mobility were angry gods. They wanted sacrifice. A Lime scooter rider rented his rechargeable device, raced down the protected bike lane as was his right, saw the trash truck trying to squeeze through on the last glimmer of orange on the changing light at the intersection and, willfully, hurled himself under its back wheels.

ON RULES

The rear wheels of a thirty ton trash truck make the identification of a one hundred and eighty pound body challenging. Truth Pedaler had been a prolific poster on NextDoor and there was a flurry of amateur detective work about who was behind the alias. The deceased had no license, of course, but his pockets were full of anti-car material carefully enclosed in zip-sealed plastic freezer bags, possibly to protect the missives from damage caused by the corporeal fluids that he rightly foresaw being squeezed out of him. The, at this point rather stained, membership cards for the local Biking Association and the Scooter Riders' Union offered final clarity, but no one had ever heard of him by his real name.

The pro- and anti-PBL crowds matched in their mutual lifestyle disdain but, to this point, their disagreements, while heated, had been essentially antiseptic. No one had been condemning anyone in particular – it was one generic view facing off against another. With this death, however, it was suddenly revealed that the passion of a crowd is made up from passionate individuals and that, while they should feel bolstered by the collective faith, they should also contribute to it. The cause protected its adherents with the shield of righteousness, but it demanded something in return – and now someone had made the biggest offering a person could make.

The shrine was constructed overnight. A white-painted ghost scooter was chained to a lamppost at the site of the self-sacrifice. Hundreds of cellophane-wrapped and already wilting gas station bouquets were propped up against the relevant garden wall. Nestling amongst the flowers, only apparent on close examination, there were a dozen or so large toy cars and trucks, each one flattened as if stamped on by a heavy boot. The shrine spoke of the sacred nature of bike lanes, consecrated as much as protected. But it also spoke of revenge.

ON RULES

The people milling around the shrine throughout the morning and afternoon of the next day hugged and rearranged the offerings, staring in pity as much as in anger at the drivers of cars and trucks waiting at the sacrificial traffic lights. Drivers no longer dared attempt any last minute maneuvers through an orange light, and so were forced to sit and accept these unspoken messages of faith and condemnation.

A Prius driver tooted in what she probably intended to be support as she waited for the green. She put her thumbs up, seemingly under the impression that going hybrid placed her amongst the saved. She was wrong. The initial uncoordinated jeers and fuck-off hand waves morphed into a single chanted slogan. Many more people joined the grieving crowd and the chants could be heard a block away.

"Two wheels rule."

4.   Hate is one of the new rules

As the gun lobbyists have known for years, the cycle of democratic politics can be harnessed in the service of extremism. Every candidate in every election has to find a novelty, a new effort, a new edge to push towards. The 'right to carry' became mainstream and there's little glamor in asserting that you're in favor of what's already been won. So 'open carry' became the signifier of authentic constitutional awareness for the next generation aspiring to be elected. Subsequent candidates were informed by their focus groups that this was no longer an exciting position, so 'mandatory carry' became the thing. MandyCarry was tested in pilot locations and found to be successful. Gun sales increased, liberals were put in the bizarre position of breaking the law unless they had a gun at their hip and, most importantly, candidates had a new battlefront on which to fight.

ON RULES

Driven by the same political campaign logic, those elected based on their support for more protected bike lanes, and for more protection for existing PBLs, escalated their proposals from punitive charges to an outright ban on private vehicle ownership. Candidates from disparate political parties showed their allegiance to the over-arching and, they hoped, distinctively edgy policy position by appending the number of wheels they supported to their political party alignment. As the incumbent candidate, Mary became Mary Johnson (D – two-wheeler) in her literature as she campaigned for the next ANC election.

Peter and Mary had reached a tacit understanding of how to share their common backyard without overlapping. He was mornings and she was evenings. During the day, he ignored her children and she ignored his spoiled dog. Peter, running for re-election to his neighboring ANC district, found one of Mary's campaign leaflets on the jointly-owned but now always singly-used patio table and saw how the game was being played. He edited his leaflet to identify him as Peter Allen (D - four-wheeler).

Cycling, driving, or scootering along any of the neighborhood streets was now a rather fraught operation. The two-wheelers flaunted their righteousness by proceeding slowly along the streets, arguing they should have priority on all types of public roadway. The four-wheelers, confident that gasoline consumption was their birthright, drove up close behind, revving their engines and enjoying every wobble the intimidatory horn-blowing produced.

Guerrilla two-wheelers stabbed the tires of parked cars with sharpened screwdrivers. The leaders of the four-wheeler resistance movement smeared dog shit on the handlebars of the rental bikes.

ON RULES

The face-offs between the two groups were initially informal and ad hoc, but became more structured as battle lines emerged. Like eighteenth century armies whose generals agreed on the day and location of their next battle, battalions of two-wheelers and four-wheelers prodded and provoked each other via Instagram to face each other down at the specified time and place. A particularly ugly skirmish outside the Post Office seemed imminent, when the intersecting chasms of race and age opened up. Older Black churchgoers, used to driving to Sunday services, had come to understand, somewhat correctly, that the two-wheelers were synonymous with younger and predominantly white and faithless gentrifiers. The police separated the opposing groups, leaving each with ugly shouting as the only way to channel for their passions.

Misinformation was rife. Two-wheelers infiltrated four-wheelers' meetings to spread false rumors that the end of the auto was nigh, and that many were already selling their cars before used vehicle prices dropped precipitously. Four-wheelers led their opponents to believe that the incidence of serious injury from bike and scooter accidents was so high, it outweighed any other health benefits.

There was no abstaining from the debate. Not having an opinion *was* an opinion. Angry activism was pervasive, more than could be contained within the narrow theologies of the two and four-wheelers, like raw sewage overflowing into rivers when the rainstorm overwhelms the treatment plant. Excited by the torrents of unprocessed outrage, cyclists threw bottles at pedestrians walking on their hard-won cycle paths. SUVs deliberately bumped cars that obtained more than ten miles per gallon for not being sufficiently pro-car. And pedestrians in the 'sidewalks are for walking' Facebook group shared videos with friends highlighting all the occasions when they had deliberately tripped a runner.

The date of Truth Pedaler's self-sacrifice had become the occasion of two distinctly different events. Each year on that solemn date, the two-wheelers formed a long line of bikes and scooters following a particularly fit young person, chosen from their ranks, who held a blazing torch high in one hand, leading to the sacred site where music played, and red wine, bread, and grievances were served all evening. Mary could see that this was a little over the top, but she and her children were present at this giving of thanks for a martyr's donation of his two-wheeled life. His sacrifice had created the opening for the imminent dawn of a car-free world. Well, city.

Despite a few misgivings, Peter attended the corresponding four wheelers' annual event, held the same evening in the one remaining parking lot in the neighborhood. Cars formed concentric circles with their headlights shining on a round podium on which invited representatives from major auto manufacturers gave their version of how the automobile made the country what it is today.

5.   Rule revision and its risks

The streets are empty. There are no cars – no one dare drive on the streets amidst the broken glass and the carefully placed boards studded with nails. There are no bikes or scooters – the decapitation caused by the piano wire that stretched across the PBL at neck height from the tree to the bus stop was the final straw. There are no pedestrians – they fear being caught in the crossfire between groups of former drivers who are hunkered down in apartments with second floor windows, righteously sniping at movements that could indicate that a two-wheeler was on the move.

Having to wait for her turn to be picked up by the National Guard in one of its new electric armored troop carriers to go the shops is undoubtedly inconvenient, but who doesn't like traffic-free silence? Mary looks out onto the back yard. It's chaotic and overgrown but the grass is verdant as there is no one and nothing to damage it. Her kids probably have too much to do on their keyboards to waste time outdoors, and Peter's lazy Jack Russell is long dead. Peter's basketball team has done well, and she might be disappointed about that, but her online flirtation with a four-wheeler from an outer suburb, a neighborhood so distant it has yet to see its first NextDoor posting asserting that other-wheelers should be burned at the stake, must be comforting. Maybe she's found herself worrying about Iran and the polar ice caps with a new awareness that what is bad can, and often does, get worse. Maybe she's thinking about leaving Peter a note suggesting that they replace the fence and see where things go from there. Maybe they are both wondering whether the other would agree that rule changes combine unhappily with blind certainty.

Richard C. McPherson

Richard C. McPherson's short stories have been called "beautifully honest," appearing in *Black Fox Literary Magazine*, *Unleash Press*, and *The Write Launch*. "Man Wanted in Cheyenne," his short story, received an award in Living Springs Publishing's international short fiction contest and appeared in their 2017 anthology, Stories Through the Ages. The rich backstory of its iconic protagonist, Jake, is now the subject of a new novel, *Man Wanted in Cheyenne*, available in paperback and Kindle at Amazon, Barnes and Noble, and Unleash Creatives.

ON RULES

Transit Authority

Monique walked the length of her empty bus and inspected underneath the seats. Sometimes the cleaning crew missed a wrapper or straw. She paused near the rear doors, noticed a smudge on a window, and wiped it off with the cloth she carried. She retraced her steps, straightened her neatly pressed gray uniform jacket and settled into the wide, worn driver's seat, which felt like it was made just for her bottom. She closed her eyes, kissed the small silver cross on her necklace, and whispered "thank you." The big bus was one of New York City's early low-emission vehicles, and its fleet number was 8521, though it was known to drivers and dispatchers simply as "Monique's Bus." She adjusted her sunglasses in the noon brightness, pressed the ignition, and listened to the Cummins 275-horsepower diesel purr to life. She wasn't shy about the word: Monique *loved* this bus. It was put into service in 2011, so was now the same age as her twelve-year-old daughter. Tending them both filled her life with purpose and pride.

Most drivers liked the late evening shift when scant traffic allowed you to go from Lincoln Center to South Ferry in 44 minutes. But Monique liked the daytime runs, an hour and twelve minutes, because she had more time to study people and the familiar but endlessly interesting Manhattan blocks. The bus followed Monique's steady guidance, like a patient, noble beast of burden, like an elephant, Monique sometimes thought, remembering everything. Some riders formed tight knots of people with few bags and many languages, headed for Penn Station trains. Others were chatty day-trippers making the long ride to the Staten Island or Statue of Liberty ferry, exploration written in their eyes. The end of the shift brought ticketholders going to Lincoln Center, dressed up nice to make it special, sometimes thanking her like a limo driver when she delivered them in front of the glittering fountain and towering glass concert halls.

*

"That's a handicapped seat, sir. Plenty of seats further back." Her voice had no edge, but Monique made sure that the offending passenger - and all those nearby - heard clearly. The scowls of passengers added authority to Monique's words. The young man smirked but stood and slouched sullenly down the aisle.

*

She first noticed the large man's off-center smile and slightly wild eyes. His Dallas Cowboys hat was on backwards and a soiled t-shirt proclaimed Don't Mess with Texas. Her eyes traveled to his jeans: they hung low enough to reveal a holster and gun. Drivers often talked about situations like this, but Monique had never confronted an armed passenger. Only once, over three years ago, had she ever switched on the emergency street-facing sign ("Call Police or 911"), in response to a nascent sexual assault in the back row. She had to act now, before he sat down.

"Sir, you can't bring that weapon on this bus."

His porcine face snarled as he leaned toward her. "Yeah? You gonna take it away, fat momma?"

"Sir, in New York, passengers can't bring weapons onto mass transit. Unless you have a special permit." Monique managed a smile while she surreptitiously pressed the Emergency Call button. "Do you have a special permit?"

ON RULES

The man guffawed. "I'm from Texas, porky, and we can carry a gun any goddamn where we want."

Monique let the bus drift into traffic, where it would block a lane, forcing honks and glances; plenty of people would see the distress sign. She knew this was an excellent police precinct where a badge or two would show up in a hurry. "Yes, sir, but you're in New York," her voice rose ever so slightly, "on my bus, and that's the law." She opened the doors, to allow people to leave out the back - and make it easier for police to enter. "Sir, you could get in serious trouble with that gun. Maybe best you step off here."

The man was startled as several people hurried out the back door. He rested his hand on his gun and glared at others who sat frozen in fear. "Maybe best?" he smirked. "Maybe best you shut that door and shut your big mouth and keep driving downtown."

Monique made a split-second decision. The man was a bully, and like all bullies was doubtless a coward at heart. He would never expect a direct physical confrontation. She unfastened her seat belt and stood, inches from the man who was still standing next to the fare box. "Now, sir, I asked you nice, but the police won't be asking." She motioned toward the side window, "Like that policeman right there." There was no policeman, but the gesture made the man look over his shoulder and Monique planted her hands on his chest and used all her 188 pounds and shove the man backwards. Hard. He fell backward, down the steps. Yelping, he landed on his back, shouting curses. Monique swiftly closed the doors, trapping the man's feet inside while he lay face-up on the street.

ON RULES

The man shouted as he struggled against the door, "Goddamn bitch, I'll get you…"

"Freeze!" A uniformed policeman hovered over the man, pointing his service revolver squarely at the man's chest. "Hands up! Don't touch your weapon! Don't even twitch."

A second officer raced to the front door and shouted, "Monique, you OK? Anybody hurt?"

Monique opened the doors, releasing the man's legs, allowing him to fall in a heap. She was shaking with adrenaline and gratitude. "We're just fine, officer, everybody's OK." The passengers burst into applause and cheers.

*

The tabloids loved it.

> *Showdown on Seventh Avenue!*
> *MTA Driver Faces Down Armed Man!*
> *Mayor Says Bus Driver 'Protected New Yorkers'!*
> *Riders Say MTA Driver Prevented Tragedy!*

The press noted a brief social media flurry, most congratulatory, but a few defending the man for exercising his "second amendment rights." The MTA and NYPD were careful to keep secret a few semiliterate threatening letters to Monique, and a pair of bullets found on an empty seat on Monique's bus.

*

ON RULES

The man's immediate plea deal allowed authorities to send him swiftly back to Texas, minus his gun, which was seized and shipped back. The last thing anyone wanted was headlines, gun-toting copycats on buses and subways, or more threats to drivers. The word came down: make this disappear fast. New York judicial machinery had rarely moved so swiftly.

Monique's supervisor introduced her to the mayor, who presented her a civilian bravery award in a private ceremony, to keep her picture out of the papers and television. She also received a firm suggestion that it would be a good time for her to get away for a bit. A leave of absence, paid, of course, had been arranged, effective immediately.

*

The three-week leave passed slowly. Monique had taken her daughter to stay with her sister in Philadelphia, where they visited the Jersey shore, shopped, and went to movies. They rode buses to the Liberty Bell and the Zoo, while she chatted with the drivers about the reliability of diesel and the weirdness of passengers. Every day she checked the New York papers online, and the story surrounding the "Showdown on the MTA" quickly faded, then disappeared. Her daughter pouted when Monique announced it was time to go back to work. She had a job to do and didn't like the feeling of shirking.

On her first day back, she settled into the driver's seat, a mystical part of her mind was certain that the bus had sensed her absence. She adjusted the mirror, traced the broad steering wheel, and pressed the ignition. She closed her eyes and sighed deeply at the faithful rumble of the engine. She released the brake with reverence, and slowly pulled onto Broadway.

ON RULES

When she reached the 32nd Street stop, drizzle began to pepper the Madison Square Garden sign and sidewalk. The sky was black, ready to pour. The bus hissed and kneeled, and the doors opened. Five passengers entered, including an old woman who looked haggard, worried, maybe even unwell. As she struggled to swipe her MTA farecard, Monique motioned for passengers to make room for her in the handicapped area.

The old woman sat, coughed, and clutched her scuffed faux-leather handbag close to her chest.

Monique started to close the doors, but waited for a young man protecting a violin case from the rain drops. He hurried aboard and thanked Monique as she closed the doors behind him and nodded. She turned on the windshield wipers then glanced toward the old woman, who had pulled a cigarette and orange Bic lighter out of her handbag. Monique's voice was kind and firm in perfectly equal measures. "Please don't light that cigarette, ma'am. There's no smoking on this bus." Nearby passengers nodded in approval, one muttering "That's right." The woman scowled but put away her cigarette. Monique gently swung the big steering wheel a quarter turn and nudged into the morning traffic. A beatific smile spread across her face.

ON RULES

Elizabeth Land Quant

Elizabeth Land Quant is a disabled, queer, autistic writer, a wife, and a mom. Elizabeth has been published in *Disability Acts*, *Red Noise Collective*, and *The Manifest-Station*, and is querying her humorous mystery novel with a queer, autistic protagonist. These poems' bones were born out of a Corporeal Writing workshop.

Prairie Madness

I needed the prairie
I needed the quiet hum of the bees
the chirping of the grasshoppers, the
rustling tall grasses undulating in the wind

years ago, it was said that immigrants
experienced "Prairie Madness" from
screaming winds that whirled around
dried up corn husks and
abandoned homesteads

but for me, the prairie was my sanctuary
from the outside world
I know now that I'm autistic
and what was so disabling
was how the world treated me.

after a school day of constant noise and
smells and touches and pain and hot and
cold temperatures and questions and
dodgeballs and bullying and trying so hard
to keep from stimming and crying

ON RULES

I would have the prairie

I could stim and not worry what
my body was doing, not worry at all
as I wandered through the pussy

willows down to the creek
the bugs and my dog the only souls
keeping me company
for with them, with the prairie,
I could be myself.

ON RULES

Unconditional

my mother said to me
your body is broken
What good are you now?

it took months for me to
understand what she meant.
What good was I to her?

my mother put the cat
I bought her to sleep,
refusing medicine
that would have helped her

costing time and money
the cat was a failure
at her utility

my husband bought an older dog
a letdown in hunting and breeding
afraid of dry leaves, wet grass, wind
her utility a failure

ON RULES

she is renamed Athena
goddess of wisdom and courage
she sleeps with a blue and white sloth
and she loves sunshine and head rubs

my sister found us a small cat
in a room marked sick and abused
someone had abandoned her when
she became a useless burden

Baby Cat is home with us now
curled up on my leg, paws stretched out
her soft fur no longer matted
her sea green eyes bright and sparkly

I watch them both enjoy their life
not dependent on usefulness
to be loved unconditionally

I put my computer down and
curl up in between them
catching the sunrays on my face

Nnadi Samuel

(he/him/his)

Nnadi Samuel holds a B.A in English & literature from the University of Benin. His works have been previously published/forthcoming in *Suburban Review, Seventh Wave Magazine, North Dakota Quarterly, Quarterly West, Common Wealth Writers, The Capilano Review, Arc Poetry, Poetry Ireland, New Orleans Review, Westerly, PRISM Magazine, The Spectacle Magazine, Carte Blanche, Existere Journal, Munster Literature* & elsewhere. A 3x Best of the Net, and 7x Pushcart Nominee. He won the Bronze prize for the Creative Future Writer's Award 2022, UK London.

My Mother's Child

Beside the utensils that groomed us amiss—
Ma forks my braid to a cornrow,
wear kitchen salt on my hormones to sugar the temper.

being comely here demands rebellion.
so, we choose instead to be fed fat for marriage.
I charcoal Ma's slender shape with hurting hands.
her image, unspooling in shaded pigment.
in place of loving my loin, I invest in knowing how this body would turn out.

a girl ago, I witness Ma zip & unzip her breath:
a deathless exercise towards wearing a sari,
while tucking in parts of her loin eaten by henna.

Ma allows me this sight.
yet, do not grant answers to the stain stewing from my lap,
to my reason for being domesticated, while our males roam freely—without
a price tag sizing them up for purchase.

all these to say, I am still my mother's child,
aware of only what Ma approves.

I go headfirst into a hijab,
in the full glare of a long line of suitors,
skin soggy in satin that reeks of camwood.

ON RULES

jettison my place, at the fireside to grow a new name.
Pa, manifesting from the backyard to greet my lack of surprise.
I've lived his name to a grudge.
my palms itch in the loathing.

I wish for the warm embrace of the males sharing my bloodline.
I say this with a conviction beyond gender,
& I would be remembered as an asset.
the dollar rates, inflating my worth.

I imagine a time when the word *woman* would be less transactional,
& a sizeable male, in the shape of fiancé—yanks the thought off like a dress.
in our leaving, a thumb press against my chest, in search of teenage temper.

I own this bile for the crime that keeps a moustache.
this heart, incapable of words.
this is how we memorize to say *speak*,
before being spoken to.

ON RULES

Male Privilege

I settle into smoke pipe, debating how we wear our boy badge wrongly.
a slaughter calls, & we participate in knives
while our better halves argue through the chiming of boiled water,
simmered hot for breakfast.

I fog my loin with blood, to raise the motion:
that a horn stuck to my wrist isn't weakness.

tomorrow, I would beg to fleece a ram
& end where the knife unmakes a heartbeat:
our lungs, softening into prayer.

I observe Pa balloon his breath to fatten the meat for kill.
he named it unmooring—as though my protest would wake the pulsing animal.
as if the word *detener** is capable of lazarusing a body.

all my life, something laid down its existence for my survival.
I've watched noble hands beat intestine into blood meal, on a platter of fat.

in one event, a wool manifests from the throat of a tray.
trembling, I uplift it towards the mouth that owns me, who turns down my
advance— the way you divert a blessing before seeking it out on your loin.

our men die, & the emptiness takes shape in plots of land.
see, how much masculinity begs the softness of earth in spite of spade,

ON RULES

till a crow answer in beak and scathing fang—thirsting over the wreck of sand
the way a labrador schemes for a final snack of meat.

lease me your finest of rams,
I am teaching myself to kill without bloodstains.
I attend to each animal with chemical stunning.

the water cants up a hotter degree.
Pa's breath flattens to one last drag, before smoke cuts off his air supply.
his trick don't do to the killing,
making him lose claim to the first gizzard as culture demands.

when meat is severed, the knife sidesteps the gall bladder: bile that it is.
I carry it in the animal of my body as male privilege.

fat collects in a tinfoil & they name it mine.
I wolf down the adipose waste, obese in the afterlife—
where Pa held his breath in my name, curious for a bone-clean sound.

*The word detener is a Spanish word for "stop".

Margaret D. Stetz

Margaret D. Stetz is the Mae and Robert Carter Professor of Women's Studies at the University of Delaware and a widely published poet. She has spent her life in higher education, but she remains haunted by her working-class childhood and youth in New York City.

The Lesson

at the crest of the swing

relaxing my grip on the rusty chains

eye-to-eye with the birds

the welcoming clouds

turning me into

Wendy/John/Michael

halfway to Neverland

to being invisible

(oh, the freedom to be

unseen!)

the weight

of my body suddenly plummeting

implacable hardness of pavement

meeting my head

then nothing

then everything

ON RULES

back into focus

scooped up like a dog in the road

set on my feet

my hands pulled along

by stronger ones

rushed to

(a hospital? too expensive)

the corner store

"Ice, please!"

shouts my mother

the man at the counter

looking over across and beyond

this cheaply dressed child

blood-soaked clumsily wadded tissues

forehead swelling and purpling

tears snot wetting her face…

I learn at that moment

ON RULES

that girls

are already invisible

"An ice? What flavor?" he asks

ON RULES

Independence

the history I learned

began in

bursts of gunfire

a blunderbuss

then musket

that obliterated

tomahawks

the volleys

sending British cannons fleeing

ships flaming at Fort Sumter

pistols, rifles sailing

Over There

a cloud of vapor

at Hiroshima

napalm burning villages

our peace and freedom

ON RULES

measured in artillery,

explosions

small wonder that

my childhood toys

were cap guns

and on the Fourth

the cherry bombs

that pitted

gardens, sidewalks

whistling rockets

gave me cover

as I crept

towards my parents' bedroom

to slide the wooden drawer

the one I never

was supposed to touch

where lay a dark

ON RULES

revolver

that I raised

in tiny shaking hands

and pointed at the world

outside

whispering to myself

I'm an

American

and this will be

my

Independence Day

ON RULES

Terry Watada

Terry Watada is a well-published writer living in Toronto. He has three novels, five poetry books (two with Mawenzi House), and a short story collection in print. His fourth novel is *Hiroshima Bomb Money* (NeWest Press). His new play, *Sakura: the Last Cherry Blossom Festival*, will premiere in the summer of 2025 during the Lighthouse Summer Theatre Festival, Port Dover, Ontario. Above all else, he considers himself a poet.

ON RULES

Rules of the Game

He pressed his police-issued revolver to my forehead. I could feel my skin depress. A perfect circle. His face flushed blood red. I shook and sweat with fear. A pitiful "why" escaped my lips. His jaw tightened; his mouth contorted into a hideous grimace. He looked like the devil.

"Why? Why? Because you're a Jap. You killed so many of my brothers in the field. You killed them all, now I kill you. That's the rule…"

Everyone liked Mac. Some may have loved him. What was there not to like? He was a cop, tall, muscular, with a big laugh. His face slumped with age, but his moustache helped to keep it up. And he was a detective, like Joe Friday of *Dragnet*, Eliot Ness of the incorruptible *Untouchables*, and Steve McGarrett of *Hawaii Five-O* fame, from all the police shows of the 1960s. These men were brave, handsome, heroic. Mac was a pillar of the community.

James Fitz McGregor or "Mac" (and not "Fitz") lived across the street from my 1960's childhood home. Like most houses in the area, his was a semi-detached two-storey with an attic and unfinished basement (my guess). Every morning, he left the house in his crisp grey suit and fedora with salt and pepper-haired wife waving goodbye from the veranda at about 8:00 am. He got in his Studebaker and drove somewhere. I never knew where work was for him.

On weekends, the gang of Ricky, brothers Garth and Craig Babbage, Ronnie, brothers Howard and Blair Trotman, and I played ball hockey or shinny in the street. We imagined ourselves to be Dave Keon, Tim Horton, Johnny Bower, George Armstrong, and a dozen others, members of the great Maple Leaf teams. Never the Canadiens, Rangers, Black Hawks, Bruins, or Red Wings. My word, that would've been traitorous.

Mac in casual attire often came out to watch us. He shouted as we scrapped and fought for the ball to score on Craig as goalie. The net, bought by his bank manager parents, stood by the curb in front of Mac's house.

Eventually Mac grabbed his stick on the veranda and joined the fray. He always complained that we weren't following "the rules" of the game. He never told us what those rules were; I suppose he felt he could demonstrate instead.

He seemed to love cross-checking, slashing, or spearing a bunch of nine-year-olds to hog the ball, maneuver around us, and fire at the net with a blistering slapshot. Craig had no chance and was not wearing much in the way of protective gear, maybe extra pants and t-shirt as padding at the most. Most times, he just dove out of the way.

Between plays, Mac took Garth aside and gave him some pointers. Garth was the fair-haired boy, taller than the rest of us with golden locks and blue eyes. Sure, Mac played favourites, but I didn't mind since we all heard. He was particularly animated showing all of the positions we should take and making plays with Garth as the star.

Back to play and Mac took pleasure, it seemed, in knocking me, Ronnie, Howard, or Blair to the ground. He liked to pick on the Black kids and the only Asian or so it seemed. Was it just my imagination? It was part of the game, I concluded at the time, maybe something in the rules I was missing.

ON RULES

It was different in the summer. We loved hanging out on the street. Summer meant freedom from school, both English and Japanese. At my immigrant parents' insistence, I enrolled in Toronto's only Japanese language school because of my inability to communicate with them. I was pretty good at speaking until I started watching TV.

I objected to going, of course. I would miss my Saturday cartoons like *Bugs Bunny* and *Quick Draw McGraw*. *The Three Stooges* as well. But when my father chimed in with a definitive order, I obeyed. Every Saturday, I got out of bed, early, to dress, eat something, and catch the Carleton Streetcar downtown to Orde Public School at McCaul and College Streets to spend three hours in a boring class listening to *Sensei* deliver the lesson for the day.

"Why do you go?" asked one of my pals.

"To pay tuition."

But summertime meant freedom. We could let our imaginations run wild. Our street ran from east to west. The south side where I lived had no garages. Didn't matter since we didn't own a car. The north side had a laneway which was lined with garages at the back of the houses and warehouses on the other side. A gravel road at the bottom of the street served as the entrance. Beside the warehouses to the west was a large dirt area nicknamed the "Dump". It was strewn with rusting automobiles, discarded wooden pallets, and other debris.

The street was ideal for road hockey in spring, fall, and winter. The Dump was good for exploring and playing soldier with our plastic guns and rifles in the summer. The Babbage boys had Mattel air rifles, unloaded, and flashy. Ricky had a realistic rifle, maybe real since his dad was an army veteran. I had a plastic pistol as did Ronny and the Trotmans, all bought on sale as birthday presents at *Kresge's*. We broke into teams. One hid in a back alleyway and the Dump. The other acted as a squad patrolling the area. Thus were the rules.

It was quite exciting walking up that lane watching out for the "enemy". We never knew where the opposing team was hiding. Every time, I noticed my breathing grew faster, deeper, my heart pounded harder, and my hands gripped my weapon tighter until it grew slippery with my sweat. It was fun to be frightened.

We were all John Wayne fighting on Okinawa or Borneo, though my team was often designated as the "Japs" (usually me, Ronny, and the Trotman brothers – being black was close enough, I suppose). I saw enough movies to know the enemy were soldiers who looked like me and my parents, but I never thought they meant me. I was a Canadian.

It was in university much later when I learned of the Japanese Canadian internment back in 1940s British Columbia. I surmised that my family and all their friends were exiled from the west coast and condemned to roam the land until they settled in Toronto. But they never talked about it. Even with my prompting and cajoling. I ended up thinking that was just the way it had to be.

When the patrol team walked into the trap, shouting and loud bangs as if shooting at each other filled the air. Garth scared the hell out of us when he loaded his rifle and shot in the air. We laughed nervously afterwards.

During a lull in the game, Ricky excitedly said, "Mac's coming!"

ON RULES

Craig peered around the corner of a garage. "Looks like he's going to work."

"On a Saturday?" I asked. "Isn't his car on the street?"

"Cops work weekends, and his car's probably in his garage," Garth surmised. "Hey, I got an idea. Let's hide and scare him when he passes by."

"Why?"

"For fun," he said with an impish smile.

Perfect for staging an ambush. So, we hid in appropriate crevices, behind debris, and up on rooftops as Mac strode up the lane.

A sense of excitement rose in me. I could see from my vantage point on a roof that he was a bit slumped probably from overwork. He looked a little shaky as he walked, not steady on his feet.

I felt the self-same heavy breathing, the knot in my stomach, the tingling in my hands as I gripped my weapon harder. I heard some of the boys snicker. A smile too etched across my face. This was going to be the best ambush yet. Then the moment came.

Brandishing my weapon, I yelled and jumped from the roof. Others revealed themselves and ran towards our prey before surrounding him.

Mac reacted reflexively, I swore, grabbed me by the front of the shirt and held me. Only me. From under his jacket, he pulled out his service revolver and pressed it against my forehead, right between my eyes. Everyone froze and said nothing. The numb silence hurt the ears.

Time stood still. Sweat instantly coated my face. My body quivered with fear. Mac breathed heavily, his face red, angry, and perhaps embarrassed. His sour breath coated my face, nauseating me.

"You wanna die?" he hissed.

I thought I heard Garth. "Mac! Mac! We didn't mean nothing. Let him go. Please!"

But he held on and didn't move the gun. I began to cry. *"Okaachan*! *Okaa…Mama*. I don't wanna die," I whispered.

"I should for all the boys I left behind on the battlefield. I should," he said finally and let go. I fell to the ground. He holstered his weapon and walked off.

I was a quivering, blubbering mess.

I never told my parents. What could they have done? They spoke very little English, and I think they were afraid of the Canadian authorities. They would have told me, if anything, to *ganbatte*, to persevere. Or it was my fault.

I never again hung out with the boys in warm weather. I never played ball hockey in the winter. I watched from the safety of my living room window. Mac joined in as usual,

ON RULES

knocking about, perhaps pushing around the Black kids even more. No one ever said anything about the incident.

A few years later, I heard on the neighbourhood grapevine that Mac had died. Probably because of a heart attack but I couldn't be sure. I stood on my veranda one sunny weekend afternoon surveying the landscape. Suddenly, a big black car drove up to Mac's house. Out stepped a handsome young man in a dark suit. He left the back door open and waited.

Out of the house stepped a grey lady in a dark dress. She was tall, slender, and elegant looking. She gingerly walked down the front steps and towards the car. I heard the young man call, "Hello Mom." Who knew Mac had a son?

They both stepped inside, the car came to life in a few seconds and drove away. I suppose they were off to the cemetery.

I felt sorry for Mac's wife and son, but my mind started to wander to all the games we played: the road hockey, the hide and seek, the summer "army" game. Yes, my mind wandered, but my thoughts always cycled back to Mac. He made up the undisclosed rules, and we followed them; at least, me and the Trotman brothers did. And we always lost, always will… That was the game.

Tom Wayman

Tom Wayman received British Columbia's 2022 George Woodcock Award for Lifetime Achievement in the Literary Arts. His newest collections are: in the US, *Built to Take It* (Lynx House P, 2014), and in Canada, *Watching a Man Break a Dog's Back: Poems For a Dark Time* (Harbour, 2020), which won the 2023 Western Canada Jewish Book Award for poetry. Two books are forthcoming in 2024: a memoir, *The Road to Appledore, or How I Went Back to the Land Without Ever Having Lived There in the First Place* (Harbour) and a collection of poems, *How Can You Live Here?* (Frontenac House).

ON RULES

The Contagion in the Countryside: Hands

Abruptly, many employed hands
were declared suspect and incarcerated without trial

within gloves, forced to endure long days
on work detail, their jail time

mitigated a little by wages
but the hands stigmatized

during any periods of parole
as likely to re-offend.

Other hands still nominally free
were pronounced by civil authorities,

despite the supposed separation of
Church and State,

as inclined to sin.
Preemptive penance was decreed:

having to wash in sanctified water
each time they entered a building

ON RULES

to obtain goods or services,
or, at these hands' jobsites,

in advance of touching anything.
For all hands, contact

was strictly forbidden
between any set of fingers and

those belonging to another,
between palms and

palms. In secret, though,
hand whispered to hand about

the effects of the repeated daily abasements
inflicted on them:

their chapped and roughened skin
mute evidence of how the constant labelling of them

as unworthy
that was implied by mass imprisonment,

ON RULES

stipulated cleansing and forced isolation
had coarsened their outward appearance

no less than their sense of self.
They remained unrepentant, resentful,

and surly,
waiting for a pronouncement

to release them from all strictures, and permit them
to return to a life

before they were regarded
as a peril to society.

ON RULES

The Contagion in the Countryside: Protocols

after the child's game "Simon Says"

The authorities said *The virus says
put your hands on your hips*

The authorities said *The virus says
raise your arms over your head*

The authorities said *Lean to your left*
and then *Wrong*

*Unless the virus says to, you don't do it
We'll try again*

The authorities said *The virus says
touch your nose with your right pointer finger*

The authorities said *The virus says
touch your nose with your left pointer finger*

The authorities said *Touch your nose with
both those fingers*

Then *Wrong: unless the virus says to,* don't
How hard is this to understand?

135

ON RULES

They said the virus wanted us to
shuffle in a complete circle

clockwise
followed by shuffling in a circle counter-clockwise

This was followed by the command
to leap into the air

and immediately those who jumped
where chastised because the virus

hadn't specified this maneuver
Yet most of those listening

had become wary
and, correctly, hadn't budged

The authorities' next requests
followed without delay

and even the overly anxious to please
now had learned some caution, didn't respond

automatically
However, a handful in the audience

ON RULES

announced that henceforth they
would obtain instructions

direct from the virus
despite their lack of training in

and comprehension of
its language, or any ability to

interpret its intent
These people assured each other

the authorities had a secret wish
concerning the virus

which only the clear-sighted such as themselves
could discern

We'll tell you what the virus needs
they insisted

If it really exists
or has anything to say at all

ON RULES

Offering

I was drawn to a November raindrop
suspended from an empty maple twig:
a brilliant sphere
whose threshold I was reluctant to
cross, afraid it was a planet
composed entirely of water.

But when at last I held my breath
and in one terrifying instant
pushed through the membrane,
I stood dry in a narrow
chapel or sanctuary
or tunnel, bright with the glow
of walls of translucent quartz.
Relieved, I could glimpse ahead
panels on the walls that,
when I approached along a smooth stone floor,
displayed inlays of chalcedony
and celestite
depicting roses, then a tree with
triangular leaves like aspen.
A short distance farther, the passage
turned sharply right

ON RULES

and I entered a room brighter yet
where on a small table
covered by a shimmering white cloth,
a crystal chalice
radiated light into a space
already fiercely luminous.

As I neared the cup, I felt it held
or broadcast the beneficent confidence
of a sage or
saint. Yet my fingers and palm
when I reached for the vessel
passed through it
as though its shape transformed to water
and solidified again
behind my hand's travel.

                  Some deep flaw,
a self-absorption or other moral failing
I'd demonstrated in my life
meant I could not lift the cup,
acquire the weightless
burden it granted.
I could only venerate
this offering. My fear,

ON RULES

the beauty of the
shining walls, my persistence
were all I took back across
the border of the water drop
to the bare twig,
the imminent
winter.

Other offerings from *Unleash Press*

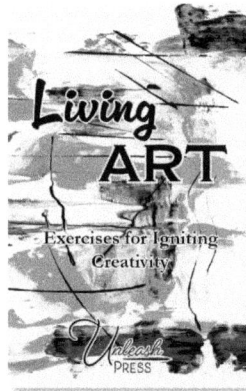

A few prompts from Create & Curate

- *"I quit." Your protagonist is leaving a long-time career.*
- *"No one ever told me…" Begin a story with this line. When you run out of things to say, begin again with the same phrase. Repeat a third time.*
- *The equinox was supposed to be about balance, but when the bonfire took over, everything changed.*
- *Who needs a horoscope? The planets told her what to do.*

WRITE! 500 prompts for artists and writers at ***unleashcreatives.com***

About the Editors

Jen Knox is an educator and storyteller who teaches writing, leadership, and meditation. She is the author of *We Arrive Uninvited* and *The Glass City*, which won the Press Americana Prize for Prose. Her short fiction and nonfiction can be found *Five South, McSweeney's Internet Quarterly, The Saturday Evening Post,* and more. Jen recently received a grant from the Ohio Arts Council to support the completion of a collection of essays on her day jobs from ages fourteen to twenty-two.

A self-proclaimed logophile and devourer of books, **Ashley Holloway** teaches writing classes and healthcare leadership in Calgary, AB. She writes in a variety of genres with work appearing across Canada and the US and has co-authored three books (with Jen Knox!). Ashley is an editor for Unleash Creatives and her work has been nominated for the Pushcart Prize.

Milton Keynes UK
Ingram Content Group UK Ltd.
UKHW011102120824
446845UK00007B/29